# Secret
# Under the Sea

by GORDON R. DICKSON

*Cover design by DOM LUPO*
*Illustrated by JO ANN STOVER*

**SCHOLASTIC BOOK SERVICES**
NEW YORK • TORONTO • LONDON • AUCKLAND • SYDNEY • TOKYO

To all dolphins, wherever they
may swim.

ISBN: 0-590-08588-3

Copyright © 1960 by Gordon R. Dickson. This edition is published by Scholastic Book Services, a division of Scholastic Magazines, Inc., by arrangement
with Holt, Rinehart and Winston, Inc.

23 22 21 20 19 18 17 16 15 14 13 12 11                    9/7 0 1 2 3/8
                        Printed in U.S.A.                            11

# Contents

# The Footprints

BALTHASAR WAS UNEASY. In fact, Balthasar was scared — at least he showed every sign that he was. Robby Hoenig wondered. What was there here, in this sunny, shallow reef water of the Point Loma Research Station, to cause the big dolphin any fear? Certainly not any of the usual sharks. Balthasar was too big, too tough, and above all, too fast for them. The Greenland shark, or the great white shark — the man-eater — wouldn't be in these tropical waters. That left only the killer whale.

But killer whales were rare, too, in this part of the ocean. And, in any case, if it actually *were* a killer, Balthasar would be asking to be let into the station through the lock, five levels down, as he had once or twice before. But he had refused to come in when Robby had gone down to the control room and opened the lock for him.

Instead, Balthasar continued to patrol the underwater station, curvetting now up to the surface and
now underneath it, his slick, gray, thirteen-foot
length flashing in the sunlight every time he broke
water.

Robby stood on the surface platform by the boathouse, watching him. Robby was twelve, and would
one day be as tall as his father was. Meanwhile he
was lean as a fishing spear from the many hours he
had spent in the water, and brown from the same
tropical sun that had bleached his hair almost white.
He had grown up around salt-water research
stations like this one, for his father, Dr. Hoenig, was
a marine biologist.

His mother was a marine biologist too, but she
had given up active work in the field. Times were
not the same as they had been back in the twentieth
century. Then, a marine biologist was anyone who
cared to study the plants and animals of the seas and
oceans. But this was the year 2013, and all the
sciences had moved so fast and become so complicated that it was just not possible, as Robby's mother
said with a sigh, to do honest research and take care
of a son and a husband at the same time. One of the
two jobs had to go. Although it was quite a wrench,
she had sent in her resignation to the International
Department of Fisheries, Salt Water Research
Division, and now she concentrated on seeing that

Robby and his father got their meals on time and sleep enough to keep them going.

At the moment, however, Robby and Dr. Hoenig were on their own. Mrs. Hoenig was away on a short vacation in Hawaii, visiting her father. He was the noted marine biologist Jacob von Hoffer — the very man who had first tried the breeding and domestication of dolphins like Balthasar.

Robby frowned as Balthasar continued to swim nervously around the station. If only his mother were back from visiting Grandfather at the Marine Institute in Hawaii, he thought. She might be able to tell him what was bothering the dolphin. But on the other hand, possibly not, since after all he, Robby, knew Balthasar better than anyone else in the world, having grown up with him. Robby's parents had deliberately arranged it. It is no small thing, when swimming around in tropical oceans, to have as a companion a lightning-fast, thirteen-foot watchdog that is afraid of nothing in the seven seas except the great black-and-yellow killer whale.

Robby leaned over the railing at the edge of the platform. Below him, the round, dark mass of the station plunged away to the sandy sea floor thirty feet below. It looked like a tower under water. Through the glass-clear water he could see nothing but a few colorful small fish, some rocks, and coral.

For a moment he thought about going down to the laboratory section of the station, four floors below, and putting the whole problem in his father's hands. But his father, he remembered, was right now engaged in some rather tricky breeding experiments in experimental tank number seven. He would not like to be bothered with problems about the dolphin.

"Well," said Robby out loud to Balthasar, "I guess *I'll* have to investigate."

He stepped over to the boathouse and took from a hook his water lung. This was a marvelous little atom-powered converter that clipped around his neck like a collar and extracted oxygen from the plain sea water, making atmosphere for him to breathe steadily as he went along. The atmosphere came up from the converter at his neck, into a transparent diving mask that fitted over his face and was watertight. The result was that he was as much at home under the water as he was above it. The device had been invented by a man named Cogswell in the 1980's.

Having put on his lung, Robby simply walked off the platform into thirty feet of water, the same way he might walk off a curb. One moment he had the bright sun and the air about him, and the next moment the glass-green water had closed over his head and he found himself flying.

"Flying" was indeed the word to describe it. Wearing a lung in this clear, warm water, above the white sand of the bottom, he was floating as if he were in mid-air. Robby kicked his feet together. Swim fins spread out from the toes of his convertible sandals and sent him gliding through the water like a soaring hawk in the world above.

But Robby had no intention of making this investigation under his own power. There was a far faster way than that. He whistled through the microphone set inside his face mask, and Balthasar came shooting like a torpedo through the water to meet him. Robby reached for the two reins trailing back from the dolphin's shoulder harness, and fitted his wrists through the loops in the ends. Taking a firm grip, he whistled again, and Balthasar was off.

But not in the right direction. For Balthasar had a mind of his own, and if he did not feel like leaving the area around the station, he also certainly did not feel like having Robby leave it either. So instead of heading directly out, as Robby requested with a twitch of the reins, he spun right and spiraled down. Robby had a flashing glimpse through the underwater windows of, first, the equipment room on the top level, then his own living room on the level below, then a moment's view of his father up to his elbows in the wiring controls of experimental tank number seven on the fourth level; and finally, on the fifth level, the stand-by tanks where the Martians were. The Martians were very interesting, and ordinarily Robby never passed them by without taking a look. But right now he was too busy getting Balthasar under control.

Balthasar, like most people who have just done something they know they are not supposed to do, was right now trying to pretend that it was all a joke.

"You know better than that!" Robby told him out loud, the sound of his voice carrying through the microphone of his face mask and through the water to Balthasar's sensitive ears. Robby pulled his own head up alongside the bashful eye and grinning mouth of the dolphin. Balthasar really could not help the grin, being born with his mouth turned up. "Now go straight!"

Balthasar gave an apologetic flip of his flukes, scattering a small cloud of angelfish, and shot off on a tour of the surrounding sea bottom.

The station had been built on an undersea high spot, actually an underwater hilltop or plateau. While it was a good eight miles off the coast in the ocean, the water was really quite shallow. No place was any deeper than seventy-five feet, and in some places it was no deeper than twenty. The area was marked as "shoals" on the navigation charts, and stretched for about a mile and a half in length, and

up to half a mile across. Robby knew every inch of it like the palm of his hand. If anything out there was making Balthasar nervous, one thing was certain: it could not hide from Robby for very long.

"And if it is a killer," Robby told Balthasar, "we'll just duck back to the station and turn in the alarm. Then the Mexican Coast Guard can come capture him."

But Robby had been underwater king of the shoals around the station for so long he could not really believe that there was anything dangerous nearby.

They began to circle outward, going farther and farther each time. On the fourth circle they came around a twelve-foot spire of rock that Robby had long ago named the Castle, because of the way it looked. Beyond the Castle, the sea floor dropped another dozen feet to an open stretch of white sand some thirty feet below the surface. As they swung over this, Balthasar veered sharply.

Robby forced him back, and when the dolphin resisted, he let go of the reins and swam down himself. As he approached the stretch of white sand, he saw that there were marks on it. They looked like a line of holes, about fifteen feet apart, leading off into the dimness of the water beyond. Curiously, he swam to the nearest one and checked it. A cold feeling ran suddenly down his back. For the first time he began to feel thoroughly frightened.

The marks were not holes. They were footprints. A good four feet in length, a good half foot in depth, and with four sharper, deeper indentations along their front edge, such as claws might make.

Something — something enormous which Robby had never heard of — had gone, not swimming, but walking here across the bottom of the sea.

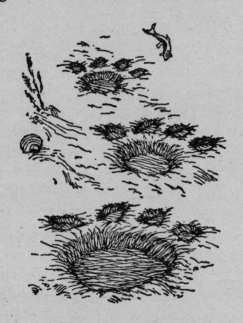

# The Unseen Singer

A CHILL gliding down his spine, Robby began, with little kicks of his swim fins, to back up along the line of footprints. Without realizing he was doing it, he had covered about ten or fifteen feet when he was bounced backward in the water by the big body of Balthasar, who immediately began to push him away.

For a second Robby tried to hold his position, but it was a little like trying to stand still on the ice of a skating rink when the sweeper truck is pushing you ahead of it. He could not escape from the point of Balthasar's nose, and the big dolphin was too strong for him to resist, so after a moment he gave in. Some people, Grandfather Hoffer included, think pushing is an instinct with the dolphins. There is even an old sailors' legend which says that if human beings will lie still in the water, porpoises will push them ashore.

So, in the end, there was nothing for Robby to do but leave. What settled the argument more than anything else was the clear sound of a bell ringing through the water. It was the warning bell of the station, calling Robby home. Perhaps Robby's father had decided that he needed Robby for something, or maybe it was time for lunch. Robby grabbed Balthasar's reins and let the relieved dolphin tow him quickly back.

At the top of the station, Robby climbed out of the water onto the platform. He hung his lung on its hook and ran down the ladder leading from the deck to the communications room below.

"Dad!" he called.

There was no answer. Guessing that his father was still on the fourth level, Robby went through the door leading to the interior stairway of the station and down three flights to the laboratory.

His father was there all right, half hidden in the temperature-control system of experimental tank number seven. The metal panel that usually covered the controls was off, and some of the system's parts were lying on the floor. Evidently things were not going very well, because his father was muttering to himself in a bad-tempered tone of voice.

"Soldering gun!" Robby heard as he came up. "Half-size temporary circuit lead-ins! Squeeze my fingers in there somehow and put the hot end of the gun — ouch!"

Robby's father backed out of the control system, blowing on his fingers, and saw Robby.

"Oh, there you are," he said. "I'm skinny enough, but not for this. Squeeze around back of the control system there and see if you can pass the leads for the stand-by thermostat through to me. Think you can make it?"

"Sure," said Robby. He slid in behind number seven. It was tight there between the tank and the wall, but he was able to move his hands and arms about where a grown man would have been as helpless as if locked in a box.

"I'm there!" called Robby. There were noises from up front as his father wormed his way in from the other side.

His voice filtered through a maze of wires and mechanical devices. "Right. Pass the leads through."

Robby found the leads to the stand-by thermostat and poked them through the clutter of equipment in front of him. He felt his father take hold at the far end, and the sharp smell of the soldering gun at work drifted back to him.

His father was still grumbling as he worked, but Robby knew his words were all directed at the temperature controls. Dr. Hoenig had a furious temper. When he had been younger, it had got him into all sorts of difficulties. Then he became interested in zoology, and later in marine biology. When he discovered how many wonderful living things there were in the world, he fell in love with them all and made a valiant effort to contain his temper.

Shortly after graduation from college, he joined a scientific expedition to explore the Mindanao Deep, a spot more than six miles deep in the ocean east of the Philippine Islands. He went down in a bathyscape to where there is no light at all, nor has there ever been, and where the weight of the water could crush a steel bank vault in two seconds. When he came up he was a changed man, and after that he only lost his temper with *things*, seldom with anything living.

Seeing life under conditions that would have destroyed him instantaneously had made him humble. He was still a hasty man, but very gentle with most people. He was also gentle with cows, horses, guinea pigs, dogs, cats, white mice, snakes, fish, and even insects and plants. He was gentle with creatures that people did not think of being gentle with, such as tigers, sour-tempered rhinoceroses, blood-thirsty weasels that kill whole henhouses full of chickens when they're not even hungry, the dangerous water buffalo, and the carrion-eating hyena. He could also be gentle with sharks.

Robby, having waited to see if his father needed him for anything else behind number seven tank, wiggled his way out again.

"There we are," said his father with satisfaction, putting the panel cover back on the controls. "Fixed.

I want you to watch that now. The temperature of
the tank water is to stay the same while I'm gone."

"Gone?" said Robby.

"Gone, departed, absent, or — by golly, that's
right," said his father, straightening up from the
panel which was now in place. "I didn't tell you.
Now, where did I put that soldering gun?"

"It's in your pocket," Robby told him.

"Oh yes. There it is. Well, what do you say to
a little lunch?" Robby's father glanced at his
wrist watch. "Great foraminifera, it's nearly three
o'clock! Well, we'll have something to eat anyway
and call it an afternoon snack. How I wish your
mother were back. She keeps track of meals better
than I do," he went on, bounding up the stairs two
steps at a time to the third level, where the kitchen
was. "Not that it makes much difference to me, but
a growing boy like you needs his food." Reaching
the kitchen, he opened the refrigerator and glanced
at Robby, who had followed him. "You're too thin."

"So are you," said Robby.

"Ah yes — but an old man like me," said Robby's father, forgetting he could chin himself eight-
een times and still swim twice as fast as Robby, "I
don't get enough exercise to require food." He
stopped, struck by a thought. "Maybe we better
eat some vegetables."

"Wouldn't a steak be quicker?" said Robby.

"True," said his father.

"And I could have a peanut-butter sandwich while I'm waiting," said Robby. "That way I'd get whatever I needed that was extra."

"Very sensible," said his father, taking a steak out of the freezer and popping it into the infrared quick-thawer. "And you can make your own sandwich, which will save me the trouble. We have," he went on, taking another look into the freezer, "been eating a lot of steaks since your mother left. I don't know what she'll say when she gets back. Particularly if she comes back while I'm gone."

"Where are you going?" asked Robby, who knew better than to risk reminding his father that he had already mentioned going away, but had never explained what he meant.

"Can't tell you, I'm sorry," said his father regretfully. "Top-secret, of course. You could have knocked me over with a feather when I got the call from Washington. Tell your mother not to worry."

"What'll I tell her when she gets back and asks all those questions?" said Robby, who had been through this sort of thing before.

"All what questions?" said his father.

"All the questions she'll ask when she gets here and finds you gone," said Robby.

"Oh, tell her I had to go someplace on government business and couldn't say where or when I'd be back — there's some steak sauce around here somewhere," said Robby's father, peering into a cupboard. And he took down a brown earthenware bottle with rings of different colors around it. The bottle contained a steak sauce Robby's father had invented himself, containing soy sauce, mustard, Worcestershire sauce, little red-hot chili peppers, beef bouillon cubes dissolved in water, and a secret Chinese herb. It was very tasty, but lit a roaring furnace in your mouth that three glasses of cold milk could not put out. Robby's father put it on his steaks by tablespoonfuls and never turned a hair or drank a drop of milk.

"Balthasar's excited about something," said Robby. He began to eat his sandwich.

"Give him some aspirin," muttered his father absently, taking the steak out of the thawer and testing it to see if it was ready yet. "Ah — just right. Now onto the grill."

"I went out to see why, and I found some footprints," Robby continued. "You should have seen how big they were."

"What continually amazes me," said his father, rubbing salt and pepper on the steak and putting it on the grill, "is the fact I can never seem to put on any weight. Not that I'd like to be fat — nobody in his right mind would. But you'd think at my age I'd have started to flesh out a bit."

"Three feet wide, anyway, and four feet long," persisted Robby.

"No one," said his father sternly, "*no one* could

ever accuse me of not *liking* to eat. I could eat steak,
for instance, until the cows come home. Of course,
now and then I get busy and miss a meal. Maybe
what I should do is set up a schedule for a well-
rounded diet. Breakfast at seven, say, consisting of
cantaloupe, corn flakes and milk, fried eggs and
sausage — and possibly a small steak. For lunch — "

"Dad, you aren't listening!" cried Robby.

"Certainly. I heard every word: you said you
want to measure Balthasar's footprint. What you'll
have to do is mix some plaster of Paris and make a
cast of one flipper — and for lunch, let's see, to-
mato soup, a healthful green salad, French fried
potatoes and — oh well, a steak. Apple pie — "

At that moment the bell that announced the arrival of a visitor rang suddenly through the station.

"Oh, there he is," said Robby's father. "Go let him
in. Now let's see — for dinner — "

"Go let who in?" asked Robby. But his father was
now busy speculating out loud whether or not there
was, after all, any good reason why he shouldn't
have steak for dinner as well, if he wanted it — or,
failing that, a good roast. Robby gave up and hurried up the stairs to the surface platform. On the
way, he found time to wonder who the visitor could
be. The boat that brought supplies to them from
the mainland was not due until the end of the week.
And it could not be his mother home again, because
his father had said, "Let *him* in." It could be Lieu-

tenant Vargas, in charge of the local Mexican Coast
Guard patrol boat, a good friend of Robby's, who
might happen to be down this way investigating a
report that Vandals were in the vicinity. In fact,
Robby was sure that was who it must be.

But when he burst out onto the surface platform,
there was no patrol boat in sight. In fact, there was
no visiting boat to be seen. And no aircraft. No one
was in sight anywhere. Robby stared. The bell
could not have rung by itself. And then, behind
him in the boathouse, he heard a strange, raspy,
man's voice singing. The song was like no song
Robby had ever heard before. It was only a few
notes going up and down, but they made an odd
little tune that seemed to have no beginning and
no end. The tune gave Robby a shivery, sad feeling — the kind that comes over a person a long
way from home, when he sees the sun go down, and
suddenly knows how tired and hungry he is and
how far he has to go to get back home again.

This is what Robby heard:

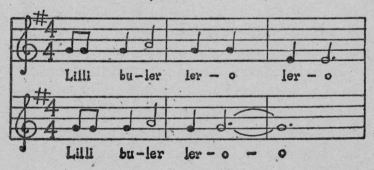

# Mr. Lillibulero

THE FIRST THING Robby did when he heard the singing was to stop in surprise. But then he walked over to the boathouse, opened its door, and stepped inside.

At first, in the sudden gloom after the brilliant tropical sunshine outside, his eyes were so dazzled that he saw nothing at all. Then his vision slowly adjusted, and a very unusual-looking man was revealed before him.

This man was hardly an inch or two taller than Robby, but he was fully grown. He was lean, wiry, and trim, dressed in slacks and a shirt of dark gray-green. He wore rubber-soled gray shoes, and from the thin gray belt threaded through the belt loops of his slacks hung a shark knife in a gray metal clip, and a flat, gray gun. Next to the gun was an olive-drab box about the size of a small transistor radio.

Some plane had evidently dropped the little man on the station. Robby wished he had looked up at the sky as he had come out. The markings on the plane might have told him where the stranger had come from.

The man's hair was curly, brown, and tight, like a skullcap above his sharp-chinned face, which was brown as well, and leathery, the way a fisherman's or a farmer's face becomes when it is exposed a lot to the sun. It was marked by a fine, curving line on each side of his mouth and a sharp, short line like an exclamation point between black eyebrows. And under those eyebrows there looked into Robby's face two green eyes so burning and bright that Robby stopped short again at the sight of them. It was then he noticed that the little man was packing something into a small, square, white case. His brown fingers flew so quickly that Robby was barely able to see a one-man copter parachute before the case was closed.

"Where did you come from?" asked Robby, without thinking. "How'd you get here?"

The little man flashed his green eyes at Robby.

"Curious, are y'not?" he said, dryly. His voice was the strangest Robby had ever heard. It had an accent that at first sounded Scottish, but on second thought also sounded Irish, only that there seemed to be the accents of other languages in it, too. It sounded, if you can imagine such a thing, like a

raspy buzz saw biting its way through a dry log.
But even with all this oddness about it, the tone of
the voice made it perfectly clear to Robby that he
had asked the wrong sort of question. Robby felt
his face grow hot.

"It's my station!" he said. "I've got a right to ask."

"Well, dinna hold y'r breath until y'get an answer, if y'dinna want to suffocate," replied the little
man, and walked out the door of the boathouse,
quite as if he owned the station, to the entrance
leading to the floor below. Robby stared, then ran
after him, tumbling down the ladder just in time to
see the man heading quickly for the floors below.

By the time he caught up, the man was setting his things down on the kitchen table. Robby's father turned from the grill with a pleased expression on his face.

"Lillibulero!" he cried.

"Ah there, James," said the little man in his rusty voice. He didn't crack a smile.

"Well, well, good to see you!" said Robby's father, shaking hands happily. "Robby, I want you to meet Mr. Lillibulero. Lillibulero, this is my son."

"Aye, we met above," said Mr. Lillibulero in a voice that said he was not impressed. "However," he held out his hand, "I'm pleased to meet you — Robertson, is it not? Y'r father's written about you."

"Everybody calls me Robby," said Robby, shaking hands without any great joy.

"Do they now?" ground out Mr. Lillibulero. "Here's one that does not."

"Mr. Lillibulero likes to use full names, Robby," said Robby's father. He turned once more to the little man. "We were just going to have a snack — sort of a late lunch. If you'd like to join us for a bite of steak — "

"I'm no slave to m'appetite, like some I could mention," creaked Mr. Lillibulero. "However, since I've had the bad chance to disturb y'at mealtime, I will join y'in a sociable cup of tea."

"Tea — tea — " said Robby's father, turning and

digging energetically into the cupboard beside the grill. "We had some around here, I know — ah, there we are!" He brought out a sealed metal-foil package. And then, rummaging in the cupboard below, produced a teapot. "Now, let's see — " he said, tearing open the metal-foil package, "I'll boil some water — "

"Dinna disturb y'self," sniffed Mr. Lillibulero, taking the package out of his hands. "An ill-made cup of tea is worse than ditchwater. I'll brew it m'self."

While this conversation was going on, Robby was staring at his father. Dr. Hoenig showed no signs of being even slightly annoyed at Mr. Lillibulero's crankiness. It was almost as if he liked the way Mr. Lillibulero grumbled and snapped.

During the meal, Robby found out nothing about the strange visitor. His father and Mr. Lillibulero seemed to have known each other for a long time, although Robby could not remember his father mentioning the name. There were other men mentioned, too, whom Robby had never heard of.

"And Morrison?" asked his father between bites of steak.

"India," replied Mr. Lillibulero.

"You don't say!" said Robby's father. "I suppose the Shah Ben Dhu — "

"*That's* taken care of," said Mr. Lillibulero, darkly.

"Then what — ?"

"Our fat friend. Y'know the one."

"Still?"

"Aye."

By the time the meal was over, Robby was bursting with curiosity and resentment. The last few years he had become used to talking to his father man to man, and now the two of them — his father and this funny little man — were speaking as if he could not be trusted. Rebelliously, after the meal was over, he shoved the dishes into the disposal. Mr. Lillibulero marched out to look over the station; Robby followed his father into the bedroom.

"Now let's see," said his father, diving into the dresser, "shirts, shorts, socks, toothbrush, razor — "

"What do you have to go away for?" said Robby.

"When authority calls, I — hey!" said his father, straightening up and fixing Robby with a pair of sharp, discerning eyes. "What's wrong with you?"

"Nothing," said Robby, glowering at the bed.

"I know that kind of nothing," said his father. He sat down. "What's the matter?"

"Oh — him," said Robby. "That Mr. Lillibulero."

"What about him?"

"What's he here for, anyway?"

"Oh," said his father. "My fault. I should have explained before. He's here to look after you and the station while I'm gone."

Robby stared.

"I don't need anyone to look after me!" he cried. "And I can look after the station. I know more about it than he does!"

"You aren't being very reasonable, old boy," said his father mildly. "This station doesn't belong to me, you know. It's the government's, and it's worth half a million dollars — or more, if you try to figure how much it'd cost to replace the Martians downstairs. I don't think the International Department of Fisheries would take very well to the idea of my leaving it in the hands of a twelve-year-old boy, even if said twelve-year-old happens to be the eminent Robertson Allan Hoenig."

Being wrong made Robby even more furious.

"Well," he burst out, "at least they might have sent somebody useful instead of a squeaky little sorehead like that!"

"All right, now stop right there!" Robby heard a note of anger suddenly come into his father's voice, and saw that his eyes had gone hard and stern. "I never thought I'd hear a son of mine talking like a Vandal."

"I'm not talking like a Vandal," muttered Robby.

"Oh, aren't you? Suppose," said his father, "you tell me just what a Vandal is."

"They're people who like making trouble," said Robby, painfully.

"But *why* do they like making trouble?" demanded Dr. Hoenig.

"They just do," said Robby.

"There's a lot more to it than that," his father said, "as you're now old enough to realize. Nobody does anything without a reason. If you get mad at somebody, you have a reason for getting mad, haven't you?"

"Well, sure," Robby answered.

"Of course you do," said Dr. Hoenig. "And in just the same way the Vandals have their reason for acting as they do. They're men — and some women too — who've refused to grow up in one particular way."

"You mean they're *little?*" said Robby. "But everybody always said — "

"It's inside that they've refused to grow up," Dr. Hoenig said. "Most people learn somewhere along the line that they sometimes have to put other people's feelings or wishes ahead of their own if the world is going to run smoothly. The Vandals never have, and they never do. They do nothing except what they want, all the time."

"That doesn't sound so bad," said Robby.

"You'll see how bad it is when you run into some Vandals — if you ever do. People who act like that never have any friends. And that makes them unhappy, which is why they band together to smash and destroy things."

"There's a lot more to it than that," said Robby. "In school — "

"I know," said Dr. Hoenig. "In school they give you the history of it. They tell you how the Vandals grew out of the old criminal gangs and societies of the twentieth century. With better methods of catching criminals, ordinary crime was stopped, as war has been stopped nowadays. The real criminals are all caught and cured now before they can get started. But the merely unhappy people are still with us. They gang up and hunt for something to hate, to prove that, bad as they are, there is something that is worse. And when they find it, they band together and try to destroy it."

"Well, anyway," said Robby, rebelliously, "I'm no Vandal."

"Don't be so sure," said Dr. Hoenig. "We're all likely to act like Vandals on occasion, unless we watch ourselves. You may not like Mr. Lillibulero — that's your privilege — but that doesn't excuse you for telling lies about him."

"They weren't lies. They —" Robby broke off, and bit his lip.

"Of course they were," said his father, calmly. "How do you know he's a squeaky little sorehead? You don't, of course. You just made that up because you'd *like* to think he is a squeaky little sorehead. Then you'd have an excuse for not liking him."

"Well, he's certainly not very polite!" said Robby.

"No," said Dr. Hoenig slowly and thoughtfully,

pursing his lips, "Mr. Lillibulero is *not* very polite. But as you grow up, you'll learn that sometimes there are reasons for people being the way they are that go a long way toward excusing their faults."

"Such as?" said Robby. "Just tell me one thing!"

"Well," said his father, "for one thing, Mr. Lillibulero was an orphan. And for another, he is a top — perhaps *the* top — security agent for the International Bureau of Police, of which I'm sure you've heard."

"Him?" said Robby. He stared at his father. "*Him?*"

"Exactly. Mr. Lillibulero," said Dr. Hoenig. "So you see, the International Bureau of Police does not share your opinion that he is a squeaky little sorehead. Nor do Vandals, ordinarily, since his main job is breaking up their gangs. And as for his being not so polite, if you grew up in all sorts of odd corners of the world, if you worked and dedicated and prepared yourself for police work, and thought it was more important to be honest than anything else, you too might be a little outspoken and inclined to say just what you think." Robby's father turned back to his luggage. "Come on now, give me a hand with this packing, because I've got to get done and on my way. They need me right away over there."

"Over where?" asked Robby, reaching for a handful of shirts.

"Just — over there," replied his father. "Hand me those shirts."

They were snapping the locks on the suitcase when the arrival bell rang. They went upstairs together and found Mr. Lillibulero already talking to a man in the uniform of the International Department of Fisheries — Fish Warden's Division. A fast-looking, two-man flying disc was resting on the water beside the platform.

Robby's father shook hands with the uniformed pilot of the disc and climbed aboard. He leaned out to wave good-bye to Robby.

"Don't forget the temperature control on number seven!" he called. Then the bubble top of the flying disc popped shut over him. The disc skimmed the surface of the water and was off into the darkening sky of the east. It was getting late in the afternoon, and the tropical sun was just about to go down.

Robby watched the disc dwindle out of sight. With it gone and the sun sinking, he felt lonelier than he had ever felt in his life. He remembered suddenly that he had never told his father about the footprints. And now there was nobody else to tell.

Except Mr. Lillibulero.

# The Vandals

M R. LILLIBULERO had already left the surface platform. When Robby entered the communications room on the floor below, he found the little man had brought his box up to the control panel for the station's signaling system and was busy connecting wires from the box to the panel.

"What —" began Robby and then closed his mouth. He was not going to ask Mr. Lillibulero another question and be made to feel foolish again.

"'Tis a specially sensitive warning device," replied Mr. Lillibulero without turning around, almost as if he had eyes in the back of his head and could also read minds. "We'll want no troublemakers sneaking in on us without warning."

"Oh, nobody could," said Robby. "Balthasar would let us know if anyone came up to the station."

"Och, aye?" said Mr. Lillibulero, turning and fixing Robby with one of his needle-sharp green glances. "And who might this Balthasar be?"

"My pet," said Robby. "He's a Risso's dolphin. One of the Hoffer dolphins. I got him from my grandfather. Actually, he's an experimental animal, but he was given to me, and he's very bright."

"Bright? Ah, that's interesting," replied Mr. Lillibulero, dryly. "And his brightness provides as fine a warning system as underwater radar wi'a twenty-mile sweep?"

"Yes!" said Robby, knowing it wasn't true.

"'Tis a meeracle of a beast," sniffed Mr. Lillibulero, disbelievingly.

"I don't care!" shouted Robby, losing his temper, which, perhaps, he had inherited from his father. "Balthasar is twice as good as any radar. I ought to know. I've had him since he was a baby!"

"Ah, indeed?" replied Mr. Lillibulero, not in the least impressed. "Well now, I'll just finish this up, and we'll go have a look at him." And he turned back to the box and the panel.

"I don't know where he is right now," muttered Robby.

"Don't y'now?" said Mr. Lillibulero. "I know where my scanner is." And he tapped his box.

Furious, Robby stamped up the stairs and pressed the button on the platform. It rang the same underwater bell that had summoned him and Balthasar home earlier in the day. For a second there was no response, and then Balthasar broke surface in the water.

"So yon's the beast," said Mr. Lillibulero's voice in Robby's ear. Robby jumped. He had not heard the little man approach behind him. Balthasar plunged and came up, rubbing his side against the edge of the platform at their feet. He opened his mouth playfully at Mr. Lillibulero.

"*Gramphidelphis griseus,*" murmured Mr. Lillibulero thoughtfully.

"*Gramphidelphis griseus X,*" Robby corrected him. "*X* for 'experimental breed.' "

"Och, aye?" said Mr. Lillibulero, still gazing at Balthasar, in a kinder voice than Robby had heard him use before. "Well, he's a fine beast, and it's no harm t'have him about."

"If he sees anyone coming, either on top of the water or under it, he butts the bell button on the air lock down on the third level," said Robby.

As he spoke, the sun, which had been slipping into the far-off waterline of the horizon, took the last few degrees of its plunge and disappeared with tropical suddenness, leaving them only the fading blue of the sky.

"Ah," said Mr. Lillibulero, squinting his green eyes at the west. "Time to button up."

Robby followed him down, closing and locking the platform hatch as he went.

"Come along, laddie," said Mr. Lillibulero. "We'll make a security check of the entire estableesh-ment." He led the way, and they made the rounds down to the stand-by tanks on the fifth level. Mr. Lillibulero looked with interest at the squid, the small basking shark, and the other creatures. But he lingered over the tank holding the Martians.

"This'll be them?" he said to Robby.

"They're the Martians," said Robby.

"Are they now?" said Mr. Lillibulero. " 'Tis interesting to obsairve they're little different from earthly creatures."

"There isn't much difference," said Robby. "Anybody who knows anything about marine biology knows there couldn't be. Their sea water isn't quite as salty as ours on earth, and there're little differences like that — but that's all."

"I wouldna say they look exactly like earthly fish and plants," commented Mr. Lillibulero, following a ribbonlike Martian with his eye as it eeled its way among some water plants remarkably like orange-colored bamboo shoots.

"That's because of the environment," said Robby. "There probably were some species quite like our fish, but all we've got is the live forms that adapted to living in underground caves and were sealed off and frozen in underground lakes. Nobody thought there was anything more than a plant or two on Mars until geologists started drilling in the dead sea bottoms and discovered the ice caves way under the ground. They didn't discover any higher Martian life forms — only these simple plants and fish that were gradually frozen as Mars cooled."

"And is that a fact, indeed now!" said Mr. Lillibulero, and moved off. Robby, his ears burning with embarrassment, realized that the small man probably already knew these things.

He did not speak to Mr. Lillibulero again, and the two went their separate ways about the process of closing up the station. What Robby did was to:

Check the temperatures on all tanks of fish.
Check the filters in the tanks.
Feed the fish whose turn it was to be fed.
Turn off the lights in the laboratory.
Tidy the kitchen.

Last of all, he made a couple of sandwiches, poured a glass of milk, took the snack to his room, and shut the door.

Meanwhile Mr. Lillibulero, with a diagram of the station in one hand, proceeded to:

Test the water intake and topside ventilators to make sure no one could get in.
Lock the first-level hatch leading to the platform above.
Secure the air lock.
Check his gun and knife.

And do eighty one-arm push-ups (forty for each arm), a hundred sit-ups, a hundred and fifty squat-jumps, two hundred deep-knee-bends, and touch his toes three hundred and one times without stopping and without bending his knees.

Then he sat down to relax in Dr. Hoenig's office, with the *Smithsonian Scientific Series*, Volume 10, on shelled invertebrates.

Robby, one level below, was also relaxing. It would have been hard *not* to relax in Robby's room, in fact, for it was very pleasant. It was shaped something like a big slice of pie, with a door where the point of the slice would be. Two walls spread out the way the edges of the slice would have run. And where the crust of the pie would have been, there was the outside wall of the station which, in the case of Robby's room, was one big window.

Along the walls were all sorts of interesting things, such as a fishing gun that worked on compressed air, the huge top shell of a sea turtle, big enough to be the shield of a knight in the Middle Ages, the jaws of a tiger shark showing several rows of teeth, a photograph of the Syrtis Major area of Mars, taken from a spaceship fifty miles above the surface, and a picture in colored chalk, rather smudgy around the edges, of Balthasar, done by Robby himself.

But the best part of Robby's room was the window. He could lie on the bed in the daytime and

look out as if into a giant aquarium full of fish and
plants of every color and size. But at night it could
be even better. There was no telling what might
come up after dark, attracted by the light of the
reading lamp, to bump its nose on the window.
After the lights were turned out, if there was a full
moon on the water above, it became even more
mysterious. Just enough light filtered down for
Robby to see the strange shapes coming and going,
and turning before the window. He could lie in bed
watching and wondering about them until his eyes
slipped closed without his even noticing it. When

he blinked them open again it was bright-green
watery, sunlit morning.

Robby ate his sandwiches and drank his milk. He
tried to read for a little while, but then decided
against it. He switched off his lights and lay in the
dark, watching the faint flickers of fish he could not
quite make out. Once Balthasar swam down and
looked in, and Robby recognized the dolphin by
his size and the outline he made against the glass.
Gradually, Robby felt himself slipping, slipping,
down that long smooth slide into sleep. His last
drowsy thought was that if not liking Mr. Lillibulero was something a Vandal might do, then he
wasn't too sure he blamed the Vandals for being
the way they were. And then Robby was asleep.

Sometime during the night he began to dream
that he was steering Balthasar through the watery
ways of a city like Venice, that used canals for
streets. No one was moving up and down the canals
except Robby and Balthasar, although on the side-
walks that ran alongside, people were busily going
to and fro. He thought he recognized some Vandals by the bushy beards which Vandals liked to
wear, but nobody else seemed to be noticing them.

Then, far away, he heard a sound like a police
siren, and his first thought was that he and Balthasar
had been speeding. He slowed down and steered
Balthasar to the side of the canal, so that the siren
could catch up with him. But the siren did not

catch up, though the noise went on and on. Looking about, he could see no sign of a police boat.

Finally he urged Balthasar ahead. They swam until they reached an intersection. There in the center, on a pedestal rising out of the water, he saw Mr. Lillibulero in a blue police uniform directing the water traffic.

"What's wrong?" Robby asked. Mr. Lillibulero reached down and took him by the shoulders.

"Up!" he snapped. "Up! Up! Wake up!"

Robby opened his eyes to find the real Mr. Lillibulero shaking him. A siren was keening through the station.

"I — I'm awake," mumbled Robby, blurrily. "I'm awake. What is it?"

"Up and out of bed, laddie," replied Mr. Lillibulero. "That's my scanner system hooting y'hear. There's a ship approaching us fast and underwater. We'll have t'abandon the station."

"But why — " said Robby, thickly. "What ship? Who's coming?"

"A submersible, Robertson," said Mr. Lillibulero. "And it's a submersible which has not called the station to warn of its arrival — as, by international marine law, it is required to do. Only Vandals would do such. And by the size of the ship on the scanner screen, it's a good-sized gang of the rascals we'll be having about our ears in the next five minutes!"

# The Killer Whale

"Y'LL HAVE T'LEAVE THE WATCH," said Mr. Lillibulero as Robby rolled out of bed and reached
automatically for his swimming trunks and sandals.
His quick fingers slipped the expansion band over
Robby's right hand, and he dropped on the dresser
the calendar watch-depth indicator that Robby had
gotten for his birthday just a few months before.

"Why?" said Robby, who was just sleepy enough
to argue.

"We can have no metal about us. They'll have
searching equipment, too," said Mr. Lillibulero.
"Dressed? Then come along. It's up to the platform
and out into the water for us, before they arrive."

"But my watch —" protested Robby, trailing
after him.

"Y'notice I've left my knife and gun as well," said
Mr. Lillibulero, slipping out the bedroom door.

"What do we have to leave for?" gasped Robby, catching up with the little man. They started up the ladder to the surface platform.

"Discretion," replied Mr. Lillibulero, not the least out of breath, "is the better part of valor. Particularly when y'r outnumbered." They emerged into the night. "It's only a wee bit after five in the morning," said Mr. Lillibulero, sniffing the darkness. "T'will be daylight in an hour. Here y'be."

He handed one of the underwater breathing lungs to Robby and slipped one on himself.

"We'd best stay t'gether," he said, and plunged into the water. Robby followed him, and the warm, nighttime sea closed over their heads.

He swam down, keeping the shape of Mr. Lillibulero before him. Out of nowhere a large, dark body rushed at them. Mr. Lillibulero swung about sharply to face it, but Robby spoke into the microphone that allowed him to talk through the face mask.

"It's Balthasar," he explained.

"Och, aye?" came back Mr. Lillibulero's voice, rather tinnily, through the water. "Keep the beastie with us, if y'can. It may be all t'our good that they dinna know we've such a creature about."

"All right," said Robby.

"Now," went on Mr. Lillibulero, "where's a close place we can hide and watch?"

Robby thought. There was Seal Rocks, a jumbled

mass of coral and rock that stuck up from the sandy bottom of the sea about fifty feet from the station. He told Mr. Lillibulero about it.

"Vairy good," said Mr. Lillibulero. They turned, Robby leading the way from memory, and swam for the rock. When it loomed up before them, they circled about it and then settled down, holding lightly on to an outcropping.

They did not have to stay there very long before things began to happen. They heard the rumble of the approaching submersible, the water tumbling away behind its powerful stern jets, while it was still some distance out. The vibration it set up touched them with a feeling like water in air, rippling over them. The rumble grew louder, the vibration increased, and suddenly they felt, rather than heard or saw, the big body of the ship come to a stop between them and the station. An underseas shock wave bounced at the rock, so that they were forced to hold on tightly to keep from being swept away.

For a moment the ship was quiet. Then there was a sudden banging and clattering as the topside hatch was flung open, and Robby could hear men jumping from it to the station platform. With a crash the platform hatch was forced back, and a second later they heard sounds inside the station.

Robby listened, considerably surprised to hear how noisy his familiar station must have seemed to

underwater creatures when something energetic
was going on inside. It was easy to forget how
quickly sound travels in water, where it has five
times the speed it has in the air, and the way it
echoes in the ear. Now, it seemed to him that the
Vandals must be tearing the station apart.

He put his mask close to Mr. Lillibulero's ear.
"What'd they want to come here for?" he asked in
a worried voice.

Mr. Lillibulero merely shook his head, as if he
were at a loss for an answer. "Quiet now, laddie,"
he murmured, and pushed off from the rock, toward the ship.

Robby and Balthasar swam after him. There is
one nice thing about creeping up on something
underwater. You can make your approach without
giving any warning whatever. On the surface, of
course, you splash. But underwater you can glide
along as quietly as an owl swooping through the
nighttime forest.

They came silently up to the submersible, looming enormous in the water. From its bottom plates
to its top plates it measured a good twenty feet or
more. If it had not been for the streamlined shape,
a ship this size would have scraped the sea bottom
here in shallow water. As it was, it had only five feet
of water above it and five below. To someone from
the twentieth century, the submersible would have
looked more like an aircraft than a submarine. In

fact that was what it most resembled, a jet plane of the 1950's, one designed for supersonic speeds, with little, stubby, back-raking wings and a long, needle nose. The submersible, however, was thicker-bodied and had a cargo section just forward of the rudder and diving planes. This section looked exactly like the rudder and the tail on an aircraft, and did the same duty.

Robby and Mr. Lillibulero approached the heavy, swelling mass of the submersible from the rear, where the large, round openings of the jet tubes were located. They skirted these, not wanting to be caught in the thrust if the motor of the submersible were suddenly turned on. They were just about to make an exploratory trip under the length of the ship when they bumped head on into a trailing cable.

The cable stretched back some distance, but soon Mr. Lillibulero came to the end of it, with Robby and Balthasar right behind him. From it waved a thin, white material which stretched over the sea bottom in enormous shreds and tatters.

"A pod!" breathed Robby.

"Aye," agreed Mr. Lillibulero.

They recognized the pod at once, although there were many people who would not have. Robby was not the son of two marine biologists for nothing. As for Mr. Lillibulero, he knew a great many more things than most people suspected.

What they were looking at had once been a device for transporting large ocean creatures without harming them. The idea behind it was simple enough. It was merely to put a big creature in a bigger bag through which sea water continually flowed as the bag was towed behind a ship like the submersible. The idea was simple, but the execution was difficult until the invention, a dozen years before, of a tough, durable plastic that could withstand the pressure of the water and the weight of even the largest whales.

What was so astonishing now were the shreds and tatters. If one of the great blue whales could not burst open such a bag, what could? Perhaps, thought Robby, it had caught on something very sharp and very hard.

"Come," said the voice of Mr. Lillibulero softly in Robby's ear. " 'Tis getting light. We'll have to hurry to see the rest of this ship."

He led the way back to the underside of the submersible. Here they ran smack into another mystery.

The bottom of the cargo section was ripped open from the inside, as if by a giant can opener.

More than this they could not see in the dark waters. Although the paleness overhead showed that dawn was on its way, the interior was black as pitch. Only the faint glimmer of self-sealing bulkheads showed where the water was locked back from the rest of the submersible, which otherwise would have flooded and sunk.

Mr. Lillibulero put his hand on Robby's arm to guide him away from the station. At that moment they were startled by a loud bubbling noise.

The bubbling came closer. And then — so close that they might have reached up and caught one of his swim fins — a swimmer thrashed by overhead. A stream of air bubbles came from a clumsy, full-size breathing helmet, and the man struggled with the painful awkwardness of someone who was decidedly unacquainted with operating underwater.

He was patrolling the side of the submersible's hull, and required the full helmet, no doubt because of the beard which most Vandals grew in order to look different from other people. The neat little lung Robby and Mr. Lillibulero were wearing could not fit tightly over a hairy face.

Robby and Mr. Lillibulero, followed by the faithful Balthasar, swam quietly off into the dimness. They passed Seal Rocks, and Mr. Lillibulero waved at Robby to keep going. About them the dark waters of night slowly and imperceptibly lightened, changing from blackish murk to a pearly gray. Almost within minutes, for the sun in the tropics comes up as fast as it goes down, it was clear, shimmering day above the sandy sea bottom again.

But by that time they were out of sight of the station. At the Castle, where Robby had discovered

the footprints the day before, Mr. Lillibulero settled down and signaled Robby to do likewise.

Robby grabbed for one of the battlements, but the moment he touched the rock Balthasar bumped him.

"No!" said Robby sharply, and tried again. Again, Balthasar shoved him away. Robby reached back behind the dolphin's head and caught hold of the harness to which the reins were anchored. He jerked quickly on it, with his "Now, stop that nonsense" signal. Balthasar backed off, but began to circle the two human beings excitedly.

"We're some eight miles from shore now, are we not?" asked Mr. Lillibulero.

"Eight miles and a bit," said Robby.

"I'm thinking about swimming ashore," nodded Mr. Lillibulero. "When I first saw yon ship approaching, I tried to get a message for help out on the phone, but on the sub they'd already blocked off our communications wi'a jammer. If I could get ashore and call the Coast Guard, now —"

"Oh, we could do that all right," said Robby eagerly.

"I wasna thinking of *we* doing it at all," replied Mr. Lillibulero. "It was *I*, I was talking about."

"But you'd need Balthasar to cross the deep water," said Robby. "And Balthasar wouldn't take you without me."

"And why would I need the beast, now?"

"To show you the way," said Robby, "and warn the sharks off, and pull you there two or three times as fast as you could swim it."

"Hmm," said Mr. Lillibulero thoughtfully, but not convinced.

"Besides," went on Robby, "what good would it do for me to stay here alone?"

"There is that," admitted the little man. His bright eyes glittered through the transparent face-plate of his mask. "It's unfortunate, y'know, about the Martians. If it weren't for that, y'could swim back to the station and let them hold y'prisoner until help arrived."

"What've the Martians got to do with it?" asked Robby.

"I'd not have said anything," said Mr. Lillibulero, "but perhaps it's best y'know, seeing the way things have turned out. There's a large to-do among some Vandal gangs to gather all things Martian that're on the earth and see them destroyed. But public opeenion will not agree — so they're at work these last few months t'prove that the Martians from the ice caves on Mars are dangerous. It was for that reason I was sent here: to guard y'r Martians. But it wasna expected the Vandals'd come in such force. Several gangs must've banded together to steal yon ship. I've no doubt they planned to kidnap y'r father and force him to work in wi'their plans — that's why they came here. And it's not impossible that, lacking y'r father, they might try t'make use of you."

Robby stared through the water at the little man.

"Was that why Dad — " he began, but Mr. Lillibulero cut him short.

"I've said enough and too much already," he replied. "Well, if there's no choice for it, there's no choice for it, and we'll all make the long swim to shore. Call in y'r Balthasar and — what ails the beast?" demanded Mr. Lillibulero, breaking off.

Balthasar was throwing himself around in the water in a frantic fashion, plainly trying to lead Robby and Mr. Lillibulero back to the station. A chilling suspicion crossed Robby's mind.

"I'm going to go up on top and take a look," he told Mr. Lillibulero. "Just a second."

He reached out, and the big dolphin came shooting to him. Robby took hold of the harness and pulled himself on to Balthasar's back.

"Up!" he ordered Balthasar. "Up and out!"

Balthasar slanted toward the surface, some twenty feet above. *He* could have gone straight up, but Robby, shot suddenly from twenty feet underwater to ordinary air pressure, would have been seriously hurt when the air in his lungs abruptly expanded to nearly twice the volume it had at twenty feet below.

When they were within a half-dozen feet of the top, Robby jerked back on the harness and gathered his feet up underneath him so that he was crouching instead of sitting on Balthasar's back. This was an old trick to both of them, but an effective one. Balthasar was about to make himself into a diving board.

The minute the dolphin felt Robby's swim fins pressing against his wide back he put on speed, made an upward turn, and broke the surface like a torpedo. All the Cetacea can jump, and like to do so — even the big whales. Balthasar was no exception. When he decided to move, he could really move; and when he pointed up instead of straight ahead, he could fling his whole thirteen feet clear of the water.

With Robby riding his back, it was not quite so easy — mainly a matter of adjusting his balance while jumping, and Balthasar had learned to do that.

So up went Balthasar, and up went Robby. And when he reached the peak of Balthasar's jump, Robby gave his own spring.

This was the point at which Robby ordinarily went into a swan dive, or a jackknife, or a cannon ball, but this particular time he was interested only in taking a look around. He jumped as high as he could, and straightened out so that he would come back down feet first, meanwhile hoping no one would be on the platform to see him.

Robby gained another three feet with his own jump, so he was able to see around quite well. He had a flashing glimpse of the blue waters on the far horizon, and the cloudless sky, and two hundred yards away the empty metal circle of the surface platform on top of the station, with the silver rudder of the submersible sticking out of the water beside it. Just as he hit the water, he caught sight of a tall, black fin cutting the waves. Then the ocean closed over his head once more.

Cold with terror, he shot downward as fast as he could swim, not minding now the painful pressure and creaking in his ears that came from too quick a descent. He reached Mr. Lillibulero, still sitting on the Castle.

"Killer!" gasped Robby.

"What's that y'say?" demanded the little man.

"A killer whale!" cried Robby. "That's what Balthasar was so scared about. And it's between us and the station!"

# The Battle
# on the Sea Bottom

ROBBY grabbed Mr. Lillibulero's arm. There was no time for arguing or explaining, and the little man wisely did not seem to expect it. Robby pulled him down and around the Castle, and in through an opening in its gray-green rock to a natural cave hollowed out of the interior. Balthasar had followed Robby through the water, and now he seemed to be at war with himself. His natural instinct told him to run — to put as much distance between himself and the great black-and-yellow killer whale as he could. But at the same time his love for Robby anchored him to where he was, even though, if the killer did come, there was little Balthasar could do to protect him. Finally Balthasar shot through the opening and joined them in the cave.

"Balthasar!" said Robby, pushing him urgently out again. "Go breathe!"

But Balthasar would not leave. Robby swam back into the cave, hunting along its roof for a high spot. When he found one, he took off his face mask and let it bubble atmosphere up into the hollow he had discovered, until he needed the mask to breathe again. Then, after a breath, he held it up once more.

"What's that y're at now?" asked the voice of Mr. Lillibulero. Robby put the mask back on. He could not talk underwater without it.

"For Balthasar," he said. "I'm collecting air for him." He pointed to the hollow where, indeed, all the air that had bubbled from his mask had caught against the rock. Little by little, Robby was building up a water-free space between the water and the roof.

"Oh, aye," said Mr. Lillibulero. "How long can the beast stay under wi'out breathing?"

"Fifteen or more minutes if he has to," said Robby. "But then, when he breathes, he needs a lot."

"What makes y'think the killer whale'll know we're about?" asked Mr. Lillibulero.

"I don't know," answered Robby, briefly, between bubblings. "They smell you or something. Like Balthasar knows when the killer's around."

Mr. Lillibulero left Robby and drifted over to the

mouth of the cave. It was not very big — Balthasar
had barely made it inside — and when they first
came in, they had hardly been able to see in the
comparative darkness. But now that their eyes had
adjusted, the cave seemed to be in shadow, while
outside the open waters seemed ablaze with sunlight.

A moment later Robby put his mask back on,
and with a flick of his swim fins swam over to join
Mr. Lillibulero.

He looked out among the rocks and coral and
occasional clumps of waving underwater vegetation. Far off, perhaps forty or fifty yards away, he
saw a great dark shape slide smoothly out from
behind one hummock of rock and coral and disap-
pear behind another. It was the killer on his vora-
cious patrol for food, and he was working their way.

For a full minute or two they did not see him.
And then he came into sight again. He had been
swimming from their right across to their left. Now
he came back from left to right, slipping easily
through the water for all his size, which they could
now see was twenty-five or thirty feet in length.
He was half again as close to them on this pass, but
he glided unhurriedly by, as if he never dreamed
that anyone was near.

But the three in the cave knew his tricky ways.
For a killer whale is not like a big shark which only
has brains enough to swim around and swallow

anything that looks like food. A killer is actually a dolphin, the largest of them all, and in the *Encyclopaedia Britannica* it says that in all the Cetacea who live out their lives in the sea, "the brain is large, its cerebral hemispheres much convoluted." That is why the Cetacea are so intelligent, and why Grandfather Hoffer had such large plans for teaching and training them.

So the killer is not merely something that can gulp one down like a sardine. He can also out-think one, if one takes it for granted that he is just another appetite with fins swimming around. The three knew very well that the killer realized they were near, even if he did not know exactly where they were.

Balthasar quivered in the rear of the cave. Robby had gone back to the bubble he was building for the dolphin to breathe. It was good-sized now, filling the hollow in the rock roof to the point where Balthasar could poke his whole head up into it. Robby put his mask back on, swam over to Balthasar, and led him back to the bubble.

Balthasar rose until the top of his head entered the bubble. A second later, a loud snorting sigh rang through the cave. Balthasar had exhaled, in the same way whales do when they spout, by blowing out the bad moist air in his lungs through the blowhole in the top of his head.

Then he sank down into the water and rose again

into the bubble several times. The bubble grew noticeably smaller, and Balthasar settled back, looking satisfied and relieved.

The killer whale swept back directly in front of the cave, his little piggy eye above the end of the grinning mouth staring intently at them. It was obvious that he was expecting them to come out — the same way seals or porpoises, or even Balthasar, would ordinarily have had to do, in order to breathe. Then he could chase them and devour them in a twinkling. Of course, the killer had a breathing problem himself, but he could pop to the surface and back down again without giving them time to escape, and this he had been doing.

Robby's and Mr. Lillibulero's and Balthasar's position was far from good. There was no fresh flow of water through the cave, and the artificial lungs were using up, at a rapid rate, all the breathable oxygen that could be made. Pretty soon Balthasar would have to breathe again. They had another safe half hour left perhaps, and then they would have to leave.

It was at this moment that something happened. The killer whale checked abruptly. His great flukes quivered a moment, and then he shot away, no longer moving with lazy power, but traveling like a torpedo, with speed and purpose. In a second he was out of sight.

Robby quickly grabbed hold of Balthasar's har-

ness and pulled the dolphin to the cave entrance.

"Go breathe!" he ordered, urgently. And this time Balthasar did not hesitate. He eeled through the mouth of the cave and shot upward. Robby and Mr. Lillibulero slipped out into the clean, fresh ocean and hung in the water, staring in the direction in which the killer had disappeared.

"We'll not be trying to get to shore now. Can y'make it to the station wi'your Balthasar, do y'think?" asked Mr. Lillibulero.

"I don't know," replied Robby. "I don't know what made the killer go off like that." He looked at Mr. Lillibulero. "Maybe I ought to go look."

"I'll not let y'do that," said Mr. Lillibulero. "The danger's too great."

"I could ride Balthasar," said Robby, as the dolphin swooped down from above. "If I saw him, I could rush back here. There was something funny about the way the killer left. Like he was going someplace special."

"I'm the one who'll go," said Mr. Lillibulero.

"But you can't ride Balthasar," said Robby. "He won't let you."

The little man paused, looking doubtfully at the big dolphin.

"Verra well," he said, finally. "Y'can go take a look. But I'm trusting y'not to go too far. Stay in sight of me, here. Then I can wave y'back if I see the killer whale myself."

"Sure. I will," said Robby, catching hold of the reins trailing from Balthasar's harness. He climbed onto the big dolphin's back and they sped off.

Robby was feeling that kind of exhilaration that comes on the heels of a close call with danger, when everything has come out all right. So now, recklessly, he headed Balthasar toward the path of the killer whale, although ordinarily he would have had far more sense. And Balthasar, as if he had given up trying to caution his young master, made no effort to turn aside from the way Robby was steering him.

They swept now into an area where the water was only fifteen or twenty feet deep, but it was also on the edge of the drop-off to the normal sea bottom, six hundred to a thousand feet down. But while this part of the reef was shallow, it was cut and sliced and gullied, and tumbled about with rock and coral, stretching clear across one end of the shoals to the Seal Rocks. It was a sort of undersea badlands.

Robby, still lightheaded, slipped off the dolphin's back.

"Stay!" he ordered. "You know the caves down here are too little for you to get into. I'll go alone."

He shoved the dolphin back when Balthasar tried to follow, and swam off.

He pushed himself through the clear water with his swim fins — not hard, but steadily, threading through spires of rock and over little white sand gullies. And so heedlessly did he go that he came finally around a pile of coraled rock and swam almost smack into the mighty flukes of the killer.

In that terrible moment Robby realized suddenly how foolish he had been. All at once, the way a drowning man is supposed to remember in his last minutes everything that happened in his life, Robby saw his recklessness in coming alone, and regretted it. But there was nothing he could do now. He had taken the fatal step, and only a miracle could save him.

And it was, indeed, a sort of miracle that did save him. For it happened that the killer was, at the moment, too busy to notice his presence. And when Robby saw why, his eyes opened wide with shock.

For the killer was engaged in a battle to the death with a creature such as Robby, who, in his twelve years had learned of many strange beasts that walked or swam or crawled through the ocean deeps, had never seen or heard of before.

# The Sea Badger

ROBBY FROZE, expecting any second that one of them would spot him. The battle was taking place on a white sand area, in a gully about twenty-five feet below him. In the corner of this arena, next to a coral cliff, stood the odd creature in a posture of defense. Above it circled the killer.

The creature did not look as if it had much chance for life and victory. True, it was huge — but it looked more clumsy than fearsome, and not at all vicious.

It had a tiny pointed head, with a large mouth that contained, not teeth, but a fringelike arrangement of broad, flat plates. In place of eyes, two long feelers trembled in the direction of the attacking killer. The thick body was mounted upright on two stumpy legs with broad, clawed feet. From a hump between the shoulder blades grew a truly tremendous pair of arms, each ending in a great spadelike claw as big as a car door. These hand-claws had blunt forward edges and shone oddly in the water, as if they were metallic.

The creature held up its hands as if to ward off the diving rush of the killer. For a second Robby thought it was just going to huddle up in fright and let itself be devoured, but then a wonderful thing happened. The killer swung in without warning, and the creature suddenly straightened. With a speed that Robby would not have believed possible underwater, the two big hands lashed out like the fists of a boxer.

The first blow spun the killer against the cliff, and the second, pinning him there, sank deep into his mid-body. The killer got away, but he shuddered and seemed to be badly hurt.

He rose clumsily through the water, reaching instinctively to the surface for air. The great spade-hands of the creature had not cut into him, but they seemed to have hurt him inside, for he paid no attention to Robby. A half roll took him to the surface some ten feet above the boy, and Robby heard him sigh as if in great pain. And at the sound Robby awoke once more to his own danger.

He turned quickly, but the creature below was hurrying off — not swimming, but loping through the water, leaving its tracks in the sea bottom. They were the same tracks Robby had discovered the

day before, near the station, when he had gone out with Balthasar. Robby stared after them.

The killer, descending once more, swam feebly, turning off toward the far edge of the shoals where the sea bottom dropped away into a green-black darkness. He swam slowly, twisted sideways, and a thin trail like gray smoke strung out behind him in the water. Robby knew that it was blood.

He stiffened. Blood in the water meant the coming of sharks, meant that it would lead the sharks to the killer — they who would never have dared to approach him while he had his full strength. There was hope for the killer yet, however, if his wounds were not too great. Out over the great silences of the ocean he stood a chance of escaping the scavenger sharks. If they pressed him too hard, he could sound six hundred feet and more below the surface, where they would not follow him if they could. And so perhaps he could survive to heal himself, and be once more the terror of the seas.

But Robby had no such way of escaping the sharks when they came. The best thing for him to do was to get away fast. He turned with a kick of his fins and swam to where he had left Balthasar. Gratefully, he caught hold of the reins and they hurried back to the Castle.

Mr. Lillibulero was waiting for them.

"Y'saw him?" were his first words.

"He's gone," said Robby, rather breathlessly, for Balthasar had been moving fast, and he had had to work to hang on against the pressure of the water. "But he was bleeding. We've got to get out of the water. There'll be sharks around."

"The rocks?" said Mr. Lillibulero. He was referring to Seal Rocks, a couple of hundred yards off across the shoals. They were called Seal Rocks, not because there were any seals around them, but because Robby thought they looked like the Seal Rocks at San Francisco, where, as everyone knows, there actually are seals.

"Yes," said Robby. "You better take one of Balthasar's reins. Hurry!"

Mr. Lillibulero caught hold, and in a very few minutes they found themselves towed across the shoals and climbing out of the sea onto the smooth water-polished rocks, out of sight of the station.

"Ah," said Mr. Lillibulero with satisfaction, as he sat down. "A wee bit of sun'll do us no, harm."

Robby found himself feeling the same way.

Human beings lose the natural heat of their bodies faster in water than in air, and swimming underwater takes quite a bit of work, in spite of the fact that it looks so easy in pictures. All this means that they get cold and tired and hungry. Robby and Mr. Lillibulero were just that. But before they let themselves rest, there were things the little man wanted to know.

"Y'ave something to tell me," Mr. Lillibulero said, looking shrewdly at Robby.

"Well . . ." Robby was embarrassed at remembering how he had almost swum right down the killer's throat. Then, as usual, he began to feel annoyed with Mr. Lillibulero. "Well," said Robby again, "I — I saw the killer. He was fighting a — I don't know what it was. A funny sort of big animal with big claws, or hands — "

"Och, aye?" said Mr. Lillibulero, his gimlet eyes hard on Robby.

"Yes, and you know what?" went on Robby eagerly, forgetting about being angry as he remembered how strange the peculiar creature had been. "I've seen the kind of tracks it made before. I saw some yesterday, close to the station."

"And y'don't know what it is?"

"It had a head like a catfish," said Robby. "And it was much bigger than Balthasar. And — and it drove off the killer!"

"What's that?" said Mr. Lillibulero, pouncing on Robby's words.

"It's true!" said Robby. "I saw it. The killer came in close, and this thing hit the killer twice — like a prize fighter. And the killer began bleeding from the mouth and swam away."

"Ah now," said Mr. Lillibulero, veiling his eyes with a thoughtful look. "Is that so?" He picked up a chip of rock that was lying nearby and scratched on the softer rock behind him. As Robby stared, a finely sketched outline of the strange creature took shape on the rock. "Was this what y'saw?"

"That's it!" cried Robby. "How did you know what it looks like?"

"Ah now —" said Mr. Lillibulero and sat for a moment, thinking. Then he turned sharply on Robby. "Can y'keep a secret?"

"Of course I can!" said Robby.

"P'raps," said Mr. Lillibulero. "However, there's little choice for it. What I'm about to tell y'is a governmental secret, and y'must hold it to y'rself."

"I will," said Robby. "Didn't I say I would?"

"Y'did not," said Mr. Lillibulero. "Not until this moment. What y'said was that y'could keep secrets, not that y'*would* keep this parteecular one. However, since y'ave promised, 'tis this. Y'r father was not the only man to be working on the creatures taken from the ice caves on Mars."

"Well, he was the only man who was doing experimental research —" began Robby, and broke off as he felt the emerald glare of Mr. Lillibulero's eyes, like sword blades, thrust him through and through. There was an uncomfortable pause.

"As I was about t'be saying," went on Mr. Lillibulero, "y'r father was *not* the only man who was doing experimental research wi'Martians. A certain well-known marine biologist by the name of Jacob von Hoffer —"

"That's my grandfather . . . go on, go on," said Robby, hurriedly, as Mr. Lillibulero's eyes blazed again.

"Jacob von Hoffer was engaged in particular research wi'certain larger creatures which have been recently discovered — and no word of it supposed to be published — in caves below those which had been previously explored. And the interesting bit about these larger creatures is that the caves in which they live are both bigger and deeper than the caves above. As a result, they are kept warm from some interior volcanic heat of the planet, for these are not caves of ice, as are the caves above, wi'the creatures frozen in them for centuries and eons, but caves of water." Mr. Lillibulero stopped and looked at Robby as if to say, "Now you may speak."

"What're — " began Robby, and hesitated.

"No," said Mr. Lillibulero. "Not whatter — *water.*"

"I know," said Robby. "I mean, I know you said water. What I meant was, what're — I mean *what are they?*"

"They, the larger Martian creatures of the lower caves," said Mr. Lillibulero solemnly, as if handing down a decision of law, "are of various sizes and types. On the average, they are bigger and further evolved than the ones in the ice caves. In short, they are the higher, more intelligent and complicated sort of creatures which would not have been able to survive if frozen in ice, the way simpler animals can."

"Oh," said Robby.

"Somehow," went on Mr. Lillibulero, "word of what y'r grandfather was doing appears to have leaked out. Three days ago, the largest of the Martians at y'r grandfather's institute was stolen away, and it was clearly a matter of abduction by Vandals."

Robby stared.

"But why would Vandals want a Martian?" he said. "Vandals don't like live things from other worlds, you said. They say they all ought to be destroyed."

"Ah. *Vandals!*" said Mr. Lillibulero, and his eyes snapped abruptly. They grew green and hard as fine emeralds. Robby blinked at the change in the little man's face, and an unexpected trickle of fear ran slowly down his spine. He would never have suspected that Mr. Lillibulero could look so dangerous. "There's all kinds of Vandals, laddie."

"Dad says they're all alike. People who just wouldn't grow up in some way."

"Aye, he's right enough," said Mr. Lillibulero. "But the way they are takes different forms. There's no great organization of them, y'see. They're just a lot of loose gangs, some of them against one thing, and some wanting to smash something else. It's

just when some of the gangs start getting together
that decent folk have to look out. And it happens
that's just what's come about in the matter of the
Martians."

"What do you mean?" asked Robby.

"I mean," said Mr. Lillibulero, "that there's one
kind of Vandal worse than all the rest, and that's the
kind that wants power. For fifty years now we've
had no wars in the world. But there are men among
the Vandals who'd like to bring war back because
that way they could become •powerful and important. Now if this sort of Vandal could get people
all worked up and arguing about the Martians, perhaps some fighting would start."

"But they don't really *mean* to hurt people, do
they?" said Robby. "And that —"

"And that excuses them, y'would say?" Mr. Lillibulero's voice was no longer friendly. "If someone
you loved drowned in the station because Vandals
blew it up, would you say it was no blame of theirs
because they were only out to destroy the Martians
and didn't mean to hurt the people who were
there, too?"

Robby, who had been just on the edge of arguing
some more, closed his mouth. He had not thought
of the matter that way. He stared out to sea, seeing
in his mind's eye the station collapsing as it was
blown up, and the tons of water rushing in on his
father, and his mother, and himself.

When he looked back at Mr. Lillibulero, he was surprised to see that the man's eyes had clouded over.

"Och, aye!" said Mr. Lillibulero, gruffly. "The Vandals have caused enough sadness and loneliness in the world to young lads without my talking about more tragedy. But to get back to more important matters. The information I'm about t'give you is top-secret, but it may be it'll help you to know it for your own protection if the Vandals get their hands on you — as they well might, with us on this rock and them in the station.

"The beast y'saw drive off the killer whale was one of y'r grandfather's Martians."

Robby stared.

"It was!" he said.

"Aye."

"But it was so big!"

" 'Tis the biggest Martian creature yet discovered," said Mr. Lillibulero. "There're only two in captivity, both in y'r grandfather's possession. Unfortunately, the Vandals that stole the one you saw also hurt the other one they left behind. That's why y'r father had to hurry off the way he did. He'll be trying now to help y'r grandfather and y'r mother save the life of the one that's left. They call the creatures," added Mr. Lillibulero, "sea badgers."

"Sea badgers?" said Robby.

"Aye. Y'see, they're not the terrible monsters the

Vandals would like to believe, for all their size. In
fact, they're vegetarian, and live on the plants that
grow in the Martian sea caves. Their mouths are
built for grinding up the plants they find, by the
bushel, and those big arms and hands are for digging from one underground sea cave to the other, in
search of food. That's why they call them sea badgers — the badger, you know, is a famous digger."

"Moles are very good at it, too," said Robby.

"And clams," said Mr. Lillibulero. "However,
we have no earthly digging creature the size or
strength of the Martian sea badger. He can literally
burrow through rock. Which," went on Mr. Lillibulero, "brings me back to the rest of the information I was about to disclose."

"What?" asked Robby.

"Down at the Intelligence Bureau we've known
what the plan of one group of Vandals has been for
some time. We learned of it shortly after it came to
our attention that news of the Martian sea badgers
had leaked out. The leader of this particular group
— they call him the Captain — planned to capture
a killer whale, turn it loose at some crowded beach,
and later blame the havoc it caused on one of the
sea badgers, escaped and loose upon the world."

"That was where the killer whale came from!"
said Robby. "They must have been towing it in the
pod — and the sea badger was locked in the cargo
section of the submersible!"

"Aye. From which he dug himself out, obviously," said Mr. Lillibulero, "and either attacked the killer whale in the pod or was attacked by him."

"*I* think he was attacked," said Robby. "The killer whale did all the attacking in the fight I saw."

"Well, whichever way it was," said Mr. Lillibulero, "they all ended up here — for what reason I'm not quite sure. It may be they were running short of Martian vegetation to feed the sea badger. Maybe it was ill, and they planned to kidnap y'r father to nurse it. A dead sea badger would not back up their lies about it, particularly if it had been dead some time."

"Well, the killer whale's gone now," said Robby.

"Aye. But there's the sea badger yet to worry about," said Mr. Lillibulero. "Or at least I must worry about it, that being m'duty. However, there's nothing to be done for the moment until we dry out and rest a wee bit. So pick y'rself a bit of shade, Robertson, and stretch out. I'll do the same."

"I wish I had something to eat," said Robby.

"I could do with a bite myself," admitted Mr. Lillibulero. "Unfortunately, we've nothing."

Robby sighed and took off his lung, and crept in under an overhang of rock that cast a little shade. He pillowed his head on the lung and went immediately to sleep. Around the rocks Balthasar swam on patrol, and Mr. Lillibulero lay gazing at the rock overhead, deep in thought.

# Into the Dark Tunnel

ROBBY was dreaming again. This time he was at an amusement park, standing by a hot-dog stand.

"Hot dogs! Free hot dogs!" the man behind the stand was chanting. "Hot, fresh, juicy, delicious hot dogs! Have a hot dog, kid?"

"Thanks," said Robby. He took the hot dog the man gave him and ate it in three bites.

"Hey, let's see you do that again!" said the man, as people began to crowd around. "Look at this, folks." He handed Robby another hot dog, and they all watched in amazement as Robby ate it in two bites. Murmurs of admiration went up.

"Hey, kid, how'd you like to work for me?" said the man, leaning over the counter to whisper in Robby's ear. "All the hot dogs you can eat and two dollars an hour. Show the folks how hot dogs ought to be eaten, and drum up business?"

"I don't mind — for an hour or two," said Robby.

"You'll have to start out by eating a dozen hot dogs in a row," warned the man.

"Huh!" said Robby. "What's a dozen hot dogs? Give me two dozen." The man served them up piping hot, and Robby polished them off without batting an eye.

"Gee, kid, how do you do it?" asked a man in the crowd.

"I've got a secret bite," Robby told them. "I call it the Robby Snap. It's the way I bring my teeth together. There's no use your trying it," he went on, as half a dozen people in the crowd rushed to order hot dogs, "nobody else in the world can do it, and it's quite dangerous if you let your teeth slip. I learned it by watching killer whales and sharks in action."

"Whew!" said the man behind the counter. "I'm having to make so many hot dogs so fast that it's getting too hot around here. I'm going to have to close down. Whew, it's hot."

And it *was* getting hot. Robby tried to wipe his forehead and scratched his hand on a rock. Surprised, he blinked open his eyes — and woke up.

The sun had moved in the sky, and the shade he had been lying in had disappeared. So had the dozens of dream hot dogs in his stomach. He felt thirsty, dizzy, headachy, in a bad humor, and very, very hollow inside. He sat up, rubbing his eyes.

Mr. Lillibulero was seated cross-legged like a Buddha, a few feet away. In front of him were a couple of white plastic jugs and several white plio-film cartons. Robby recognized them at once. They were the standard emergency rations every life-boat and small sea or aircraft had to carry under law.

"Where'd you get those?" said Robby.

"From the craft in y'r boathouse," replied Mr. Lillibulero. "I swam over and slipped in while y'were sleeping." He passed a jug and a couple of the cartons to Robby.

"Thanks," muttered Robby, looking sourly at the two objects in his hands. He knew very well what went into boat emergency rations, and was not too pleased at the prospect of eating them. What he really wanted was a triple-decker peanut-butter sandwich and an enormous tumbler of ice-cold milk.

But there was no denying that he was thirsty, so he broke the seal on the white jug and took a swallow. The water inside was warm, and it had that particular flat taste that water gets when it has been sitting so long that all the air has gone out of it. But it flowed down Robby's dry throat like lemonade. He took the jug away from his mouth and looked at it in astonishment.

After drinking the water, Robby suddenly discovered how hungry he was. He broke open the carton and dug into the rations. And these, like the water, were surprisingly delicious. To him the hard, nourishing biscuits tasted like fine, crusty French bread, the chewy bar of compressed meat tasted better than fresh-grilled hamburgers, and the cube of rich chocolate outdid all candy and desserts he had ever eaten.

Meanwhile Mr. Lillibulero had been sitting with his elbow in one hand and his chin in the other. His green eyes were veiled once more in thought. Robby opened his mouth to speak, and then — wisely — thought better of it. He waited.

After a moment, Mr. Lillibulero's expression became bright and piercing again, and he glanced over at Robby.

"Ah, Robertson," he said. "I've come to a wee decision, here. Are y'through eating?"

"I think so," said Robby, and took another swallow of water. "Yes," he said.

"Ah then, pay attention," said the little man. "We find ourselves at th'moment in a very preecarious position, y'understand. 'Caught between the devil and the deep blue sea' might weel describe it. On the one hand, prudence bids me try to swim to the mainland. On the other hand, duty calls me to remain here. And in spite of y'r Balthasar (fine beast though the creature is, I've n'doubt) I hesitate to let y'try to make the beach, y'rself."

"I could — " began Robby.

"Dinna interrupt," said Mr. Lillibulero. "As I was

in the process of saying, my duty orders me to remain here. I must try to find and, if possible, recapture yon sea badger. There may be a bit of danger involved in th'job, and I hesitate t'expose y'to it.
There y'see my dilemma — there's danger for you
if I part with you, and danger if we stay together."

"I can take care of — "

"Nobody," said Mr. Lillibulero decisively, "can
take care of himself in all situations. M'self, now,
I've had a bit of experience wi'tight spots, but I
wouldna say *I* could always take care of m'self.
However, t'get back to the point. Since y'know this
particular underwater area as well as y'do, and have
y'r friend Balthasar for company, it appears t'be
the lesser of two evils t'keep you with me. Accord-
ingly, I've decided that we hunt the sea badger
t'gether."

He paused and trowned at Robby.

"Y'will, of course, obey orders at all times, and
wi'out stopping to ask why."

Robby, who had been just about to get excited
over the prospect of hunting the sea badger, found
himself irritated instead. The idea of Mr. Lillibulero
treating him like a baby was more than he could
stand, particularly when he thought of how much
better he must know the creatures of the sea, and
the area around the underwater station, than the
little man possibly could.

"I'll be all right," Robby growled.

"See that y'are. And now," went on Mr. Lillibulero, "t'track down the sea badger. We'll be going to where y'saw it last, and follow the footprints it seems the beast has a habit of leaving."

He gathered up the pliofilm cartons and the two
water jugs, and hid them in a crevice of the rocks.
Then he adjusted his lung and slid off the rock into
the water. Robby followed, still annoyed.

They swam down through the green water, and
Balthasar came to tow them. Robby took one of the
reins of the dolphin's harness, Mr. Lillibulero took
the other, and they headed toward the place of the
battle between the killer whale and the sea badger.
Robby looked nervously around for sharks. But if
they had been attracted by the fight, they were
now at their business in other parts of the ocean.
Only a two-foot-long hammerhead shark, too small
to be dangerous, cruised along the bottom below
them.

When they reached the gully, the footprints were
no longer to be seen. The gently moving waves had
erased them from the loose, light sand.

Robby, however, pointed out the narrow gully
down which he had seen the Martian creature go.
For a while it seemed that they might be right on
the trail, but in a little while the gully became so
broken up by hollows and high spots and little val-
leys splitting off that it was soon apparent that they
were wandering about at random.

It was at this moment that Balthasar gave them a helping hand. He had been swooping and stunting about them ever since they reached the place where the fight occurred. As a swimmer, Balthasar was, compared to them, like a blooded race horse trying to hold his pace down to a humble burro's. He could literally swim rings around them, and usually did. So it seemed all the more strange, then, when he suddenly stopped doing this, and as suddenly began to push Robby back the way they had come.

"Hey!" cried Robby, excitedly, through his mask to Mr. Lillibulero. "I bet we're getting close to the sea badger — quit it, Balthasar!"

Balthasar expressed his concern with every fluke and flipper of his being.

"Now stop it, Balthasar!" said Robby. "It's perfectly harmless. It's a vegetarian Martian."

Balthasar protested.

"That's enough of that!" said Robby sharply, giving Balthasar's harness a warning jerk that ordered him to obey, no matter what. Balthasar shivered backward in the water, but did as he was told.

After a little while Robby and Mr. Lillibulero came upon the creature's tracks. They seemed to wander about without any real plan.

"Why do you suppose he's going around all over the place like this?" Robby asked Mr. Lillibulero.

"I've no idea," replied the small man briefly.

"He acts like he's looking for something," said

Robby, but he said it half to himself, and Mr. Lilli-bulero gave him no answer.

Several times they lost the trail when the sea badger walked over rocks, or where the bottom was so hard that it did not show footprints. Then they had to swim around in bigger and bigger circles until they caught sight of the tracks again.

Mr. Lillibulero was leading the way between two spires of rock when he stopped so suddenly that Robby swam into him from behind.

"What is it?" asked Robby, wiggling forward. Mr. Lillibulero caught him by the shoulder.

"Moray eel," he said.

Robby looked into a dark hollow between the rock spires. Sure enough, there, his eyes glittering above his sharp snout and snarly mouth, was a member of the family of the Muraenidae. His angry jaws gaped at them, daring them to approach too close.

"It's all right," said Robby. "I know him. If we don't come too near, he won't bother us."

Writhing and slithering about in the water, the eel cocked a bitter eye at them. It was quite true. Vicious as he is if pressed, the moray eel always has his own territory and prefers to fight on it if given his choice. For he is conservative, as a great many fish are — and fish he is, in spite of his snakelike shape and actions. The eel, whether moray, conger, or any other kind, is simply a fish grown long and limber and narrow. And in Europe, where people are more used to him, he is caught and sold in the markets and eaten in large numbers.

"However," said Mr. Lillibulero, "we'll take the long way around and risk no risks." And he led the way out from between the spires to pick up the trail beyond.

Robby followed, sneering. He was feeling unkind toward things in general. Lifeboat emergency rations and a short nap in the hot tropical sun were poor substitutes for a normal schedule of sleep and food. So this was the brave Mr. Lillibulero, thought Robby disdainfully afraid of a moray eel! This was the dangerous Mr. Lillibulero! This was the Mr. Lillibulero who was supposed to look after the station and Robby while Robby's father was gone! This was —

"Watch y'r head," warned Mr. Lillibulero, and Robby, who had been so busy thinking that he had almost swum directly into the little man's wavering swim fins, checked himself.

"Huh!" muttered Robby. "Watch your own self!" But he muttered it under his breath, and if Mr. Lillibulero heard, he ignored it.

All this time they had been following the tracks of the sea badger as they wound about the ocean floor. Now those tracks led them to a pile of underwater rock that Robby knew well. Nor did they stop at the rock. For there was in this rock a huge hole, a cavelike entrance like the opening into a tunnel. The tracks went directly in and did not come out again.

Mr. Lillibulero peered into the darkness at the mouth of the hole.

"Well," he said, at last, "I fear there's no hope for it. Y'wait here, Robertson. I'll go in and see if the beast is there now."

Robby opened his mouth to protest, then closed it again. He had just had a thought. It was something he was to regret later, but at the moment he hugged it to himself secretly.

Mr. Lillibulero swam alone into the hole.

# Alone Against the Raiders

Robby hung in the water, waiting for Mr. Lillibulero to reappear, and the moments slipped by. To occupy himself, Robby thought about his idea.

It was really not so much an idea as a piece of secret knowledge. For he happened to know that the hole in front of him was not a hole, but a tunnel in the rock. And in the tunnel was an octopus. It was not a large octopus, and Robby knew octopi are shy creatures and not really dangerous, anyway. But he was hoping that Mr. Lillibulero would not know this, and would come flying out in fear.

Floating in the water, Robby daydreamed of how he would swim to the rescue, and of how impressed Mr. Lillibulero would be. Meanwhile, no sign of Mr. Lillibulero. The minutes continued to crawl by. Balthasar, becoming bored, had swum

away, though he probably had not gone far. Now as
Robby waited, a small spiny puffer swam out of the
tunnel, saw Robby, and immediately blew itself up
in alarm. It bobbed in the water like a round little
ball studded with spikes.

"Don't be crazy," said Robby to it, "I don't eat
puffers. You think I want to get poisoned?"

The puffer backed speedily off through the water,
but remained inflated until it was a safe distance
away. Then it returned to its normal shape and
size.

Balthasar came back and nosed Robby inquir-
ingly. For the first time, Robby began to feel uncomfortable.

Mr. Lillibulero had had plenty of time — not
just to find the octopus and retreat in fright, but to
reach the far end of the tunnel and open water, and
return for Robby. But he had not come back.

Robby was now a little scared. He felt sure that
Mr. Lillibulero had run across the octopus, and
something wholly unexpected had happened. The
more Robby turned the idea over in his head, the
more worried he became.

At last Robby swam nervously into the tunnel,
unaccompanied even by Balthasar, who had wan-
dered off once more.

The tunnel's darkness enfolded him at once. It
was like swimming into absolute night. But his eyes

began to adjust quickly, and he had the advantage of knowing how the tunnel turned and twisted.

He swam on, and very soon the water began to gray and lighten as he approached the far end where the octopus should be.

Here the roof of the tunnel began to reveal openings to the water overhead. But the sunlight filtering down from above showed no octopus. And no Mr. Lillibulero. What it did show was something frighteningly different. Just ahead, where the end of the tunnel was choked by coral, sand, and rock ripped from the tunnel floor, a gaping hole opened in the ocean bed. The hole was so deep and dark that Robby could make out nothing in it. But in the soft sand and rubble in front of it, there was a deep print — the heavy mark of the sea badger's clawed foot. The footprint pointed into the hole. There was nothing pointing out again.

Robby found himself swimming, panic-stricken, as fast as he could. He burst out the entrance to the tunnel, almost blundering into Balthasar, who was now waiting there for him. He grabbed at the reins and flipped them. Balthasar spun about with a swirl of the water and raced off, trailing Robby behind him.

Robby torpedoed through the water. As he put a little distance between himself and the tunnel, his panic began to grow less. It ebbed from his mind, leaving behind the almost as frightening fact that Mr. Lillibulero and the sea badger must be down there in that hole together. The footprint Robby had seen showed that the Martian creature had gone in and not come out again. Mr. Lillibulero had also gone in. There was no place else for him to be, with the far end of the tunnel blocked the way it was. Mr. Lillibulero would certainly have come back by this time, Robby thought. That is, if he were able to come back.

Robby could feel his heart throbbing like a propeller. Mr. Lillibulero was in serious trouble, and there was no one but Robby to do anything about it. For a moment Robby thought wildly of going to the Vandals in the station, giving himself up, and begging them to rescue Mr. Lillibulero. It would mean, of course, that the Vandals would be able to recapture the sea badger after all. But human life, Robby's father had always said, was sacred. Mr. Lillibulero — or any person, for that matter — was more important than the Martian.

That is, thought Robby, if Mr. Lillibulero were still all right. A creature like the sea badger that could drive off a killer whale could do just about anything it liked to a single human swimmer.

Then, unexpectedly, Robby remembered something. There had been no sign of sharks around the tunnel entrance. That meant that, whatever else had happened, Mr. Lillibulero had not been wounded by the sea badger. Sharks could scent blood in the water from great distances, and they would have been on the spot by this time, hoping to finish off whatever was there.

So at least Mr. Lillibulero had not been hurt. And aside from that, he should be fairly safe for the moment. His face mask would go on manufacturing oxygen from the water around him, and the hole looked big enough for there to be plenty of fresh water circulating into it. But, thought Robby unhappily, he could not stay where he was forever, underwater without food or rest. And there was no telling what a strange being like the sea badger might be up to. It could have dug the hole to make itself a nest. It might even be planning to hibernate, to save its strength, since it was cut off from its usual sources of food.

Robby suddenly straightened up in the water. Why, he wondered, hadn't he or Mr. Lillibulero thought of it before? It was the most sensible reason anyone could imagine for the way the sea badger had been prowling around. Being a Martian, it would probably not eat any of the earthly sea plants any more than the Martians in the station tanks had ever been able to do. It would need Martian vegetation. And if that were the case, Robby thought he knew how he could lure the sea badger out of the hole and give Mr. Lullibulero a chance to escape.

Then, once the little man was free, he could do the deciding about what the two of them would do

next. Robby made himself a silent promise that
from now on he would let Mr. Lillibulero make the
decisions for both of them. From now on, that is,
as soon as Mr. Lillibulero was free. Robby twitched
at Balthasar's reins and headed the dolphin toward
the station.

They came in low, skimming the sea bottom,
with Robby keeping a wary eye cocked for Vandal
swimmers in the water. But there were none to be
seen. He aimed for the salt-water intake on the
fifth level. A gentle current helped him into it.

The opening was too small for Balthasar, and it
would have been cramped for a grown man, but
Robby could travel along it very well. He swam
through the intake to the pumping chamber, circled the screen around the pump with only a little
difficulty, and turned down the conduit leading to
the tank that held the station's Martians.

Where the conduit joined this tank, it was
equipped with a complicated filter-mixer which
made sure the sea water was altered to conform in
every way to the slightly different sort of sea water
found in the Martian caves. To open the tank entrance, as Robby planned to do, would be to mix
this special water with ordinary sea water. But
Robby reminded himself that the sea badger seemed
to live in earth's ocean water well enough, so possibly it would be all right for the other Martians.
The openings were set up to be handled easily for

maintenance purposes, and Robby got them un-
done without any trouble.

It gave Robby a quivery feeling actually to be
in there with the Martians, as if he were one of the
specimens himself. He had looked through the
glass walls of the tanks from the other side so many
times that he could imagine how he must appear,
swimming around inside. Several small, ribbon-
shaped creatures took alarm as he approached, and
they dashed off to hide, much as their earthly cous-
ins might have done in a similar situation. But
Robby ignored them. He was busy pulling up large
handfuls of the delicate, bamboolike Martian plants.
When he had an armload, he swam out of the

tank with it, carefully locking the entrance again behind him, and headed back toward the outside of the station. A few stems floated out of his arms as he went and settled to the bottom of the conduit, but he was able to hold on to most of what he had. He reached the pumping chamber, and, with a small struggle against the incoming current, he made it out the intake pipe into the open sea.

Balthasar was glad to see him, and curious about the vegetation. Robby pushed aside the dolphin's inquiring head and grasped his reins. He steered Balthasar away from the station, leaving a trail of the plants, which sank to the sea bottom. Like the sea badgers, most of the Martian plants seemed to be heavier than their earthly counterparts. This was odd, since the gravity on Mars is much less, and one would expect Martian natives to be rather flimsy and light. It was thought that temperature-induced currents in the underground Martian seas might in part be responsible, too. But Robby had no time to think about that now. He was too busy.

When he dropped the last plant, he checked Balthasar and turned the dolphin back. Now that the job was done, he remembered again, in a rush, how hungry and weary he was.

He had just recalled the boat in the boathouse from which Mr. Lillibulero got the emergency rations. There would be still more food and water in the lockers. All he had to do was sneak in and

get it. He could swim in underwater, climb directly
into the boat itself, then eat, drink, and hide there
until the sea badger released Mr. Lillibulero. Perhaps Mr. Lillibulero could start the boat without
the key, and they could scoot for shore.

All was quiet from within the station as he carefully floated up underneath the boathouse. The
water darkened around him as the boat's shadow
came between him and the sun. He rose, and his
head broke water beside the boat, tied to the four
bits that anchored it. The room echoed to the
gentle lapping of the little waves in the dimness of
the boathouse. Robby reached for the side of the
boat to pull himself aboard, and the hull bumped
loudly against the bits. Robby froze. But no sound
of alarm came from the platform outside. Rapidly
changing his mind, he swam over to the end of
the boathouse where the platform built around the
three sides of the boat was open to let a swimmer
climb up. He grabbed hold and hoisted himself
out of the water. It was an effort, for he was tired.

At last he stood upright in the fresh air. His legs
trembled a little with his own weight. But before he
could take a step toward the boat, the door at the
end of the boathouse opened behind him.

Strong arms clamped suddenly around him, catching him. A man's voice yelled in his ear.

"Harry! Charlie! Come quick. I caught one of
them!"

# In the Hands of the Vandals

ROUGH HANDS hauled Robby out onto the platform. For a moment the bright sun dazzled him. Then he saw a big, bushy-bearded face looming before him. Twisting his head, he saw another similar beard on the face of the man holding him. Both men were big. In blue zippered jackets and white trousers, they looked fierce. Robby tried to tell himself that he wasn't frightened, but his heart thudded in his chest.

"It's just a kid," said the one in front of Robby.

"That's all right!" said the one holding him. "It's still one of them. The Captain'll be glad to see him. Where's Charlie?"

"He went back down. Bring the boy along. Captain's in the office downstairs." He shoved his bushy face down toward Robby. "Where is everybody? Where's your folks?"

"They're g-gone," stammered Robby.

"Never mind *you* asking him questions, Harry!" interrupted the Vandal holding Robby. "Captain'll ask the questions. Come on, kid!"

He walked Robby forward to the entrance. They all descended together, Robby first, the Vandal who had captured him right behind, and the one named Harry bringing up the rear. As they marched down to the library office, Robby had a chance to see that whatever else the Vandals were, they were not good housekeepers. There were full ash trays everywhere and lots of candy wrappers wadded up and dropped carelessly on the floor.

At the door of the office they knocked. The door opened, and a blond boy about sixteen years old looked out. His hair was uncombed, and he had a few scraggly hairs on his face. His eyes widened as he saw Robby.

"Hey, Jones," said the Vandal holding Robby, "I got a prisoner for the Captain."

"Bring him in! Bring him in!" barked a voice from within the office. Robby was thrust into the room.

He found himself standing before his father's desk. Behind the desk was a short, angry-looking man with a jutting chin, freckles, and a red beard.

"Well," he said, staring at Robby, "well, well. Where're your people?" The last words shot out as from a gun.

"P-people?" gulped Robby.

"Your family — your father and mother?"

"They're gone," said Robby faintly.

"Gone? Gone where? Gone when?"

Robby falteringly explained that his mother was on vacation and his father had left the day before.

"You better tell me the truth!" said the red-bearded Vandal captain, leaning over the desk to shake a finger in Robby's face. "You're sure they're gone?"

Robby nodded.

"Where've you been all this time?"

"In the water," said Robby, "swimming." Just then he happened to catch the eye of the blond boy, who had come around to stand behind the Captain. The blond boy gave him a horrible grin over the Captain's shoulder, and drew one finger slowly across his throat. Robby's heart flip-flopped, and the Captain, probably warned by the expression on Robby's face, turned around in time to catch the blond boy in the act.

"*Jones!*" roared the Captain. The blond boy shivered, all the sly fun going out of his face. The Captain jerked his head back to Robby, and his gaze rested on Robby's swimming trunks, lung, and mask.

"Lock him in his room!" he roared. "Everybody out! I want the water around this station searched with a magnifying glass!"

Robby was hustled out and down to the living section on the floor below. The door to his own room slammed behind him, and he heard the click of the lock.

He fell on his own bed, and tears sprang to his eyes. He did not know what the Vandals were going to do with him, or if they would ever let him see his father and mother again. But in spite of his fears, he slept from sheer exhaustion.

Robby woke with a start. Bright-green undersea daylight poured in the big window of his bedroom. He sat up, rubbing at his eyes. The bed was rumpled, the covers thrown back, and his lung and mask were lying on the floor. Vaguely, he remembered waking up in the nighttime, after having fallen asleep on the bed, and taking them off. A bump on the window made him look up.

Balthasar was stunting outside, trying to get his attention. Robby gave the dolphin an automatic wave and got up.

He dressed himself in shorts and a striped T shirt. It was good to get out of his swimming trunks, which felt as if they had almost grown to him after a night and a day of continuous wearing. Once dressed, Robby became conscious that he was very hungry. The Vandals had evidently not taken the trouble to wake him up for dinner.

He went over and tried the door, but it was locked. He pounded on it, and shouted a few times, but nothing happened. After a moment, he had an idea. He walked to the phone beside his bed. He

knew he could not call out of the station. Mr. Lillibulero had said the communications were jammed.
But he thought he might be able to raise someone
inside the station.

He pressed the first in a row of buttons that were
lined up below that blank gray screen on his phone,
but the foot-square area of it did not light up. In
rapid succession, he tried the buttons for the various rooms, starting at the top of the station and
working down. It was not until he pressed the button for the library office that the screen suddenly
lighted up, and he saw the jutting chin and red hair
of the Vandal captain staring at him.

"Who's that? Oh, it's you!" said the Captain.
"What're you doing, using the phone?"

"I'm hungry," said Robby.

"Oh? We'll see about that!" said the Captain,
and broke the connection from his end. Robby sat
back from his own phone, feeling quivery inside,
wondering if it might not have been better to go on
being hungry rather than arouse the Captain.

After several minutes, however, the door to his
room was unlocked. It opened to show the blond
boy, who took Robby up to the kitchen and stood
over him while he fixed himself bacon and eggs.

"Now," said the blond boy when Robby was done
and the dishes put in the disposal, "Captain wants
to see you."

He took Robby up to the library office and pushed

him in, closing the door behind him. Robby found himself alone with the Captain, who was sitting at the desk. The Captain looked up at Robby and smiled.

"Come in, come in," he said. "Sit down." Robby came forward and eased himself into a chair beside the desk, facing the Captain. The Captain was showing two rows of white teeth in his red beard, but somehow Robby did not feel that his smile was genuine.

"Well, well," said the Captain, still smiling. "I've been looking around here." He waved his hand at the filing cabinet that held his father's personal papers and records. "So you're young Robin."

"Robertson," mumbled Robby.

"Don't they call you Robin for short? Well, now," said the Captain, leaning forward with his elbows on the desk, "Robertson, that was too bad about your not getting any dinner last night. That Jones can't remember a thing. But then he's not good for much, anyway. I can see just by looking at you, you're several times smarter than he is."

There seemed to be hardly anything to say to this, so Robby did not reply.

"If I didn't realize you were a bright one, I wouldn't waste my time talking to you like this, of course," said the Captain. "But I think there's some hope of your understanding things. I don't like the thought of a bright boy like you having to live with

all the wrong notions people spread around nowadays." He winked at Robby.

"You know, all those stories about Vandals?"
He laughed. "Yes, I can see you do. Well now, I'm
going to tell you something that will knock you
right out of that chair you're sitting in." He pointed
a freckled finger at Robby. "Some of those stories
are true!"

He sat back and nodded seriously.

"It's a fact!" he said. "Now, what do you think
of that?" Robby was feeling bewildered. So far
the Captain had carried on the conversation all by
himself, and none of it seemed to make much sense.
But he saw now that the Captain had finally stopped
and was waiting for an answer.

"I don't know," he managed, finally.

"Of course you don't," said the Captain. "How
could you? How could you tell the true stories from
the false ones? Lots of well-educated people —
even your father and mother, I'll bet — haven't any
way of telling the true stories from the lies. Yes,
Robin," he said, leaning forward again, "there are
some Vandals who do terrible things. But there
are others," he paused and tapped himself sig-
nificantly on the chest of his blue zippered jacket,
"who are simply working for the good of all men.
You understand me?" He paused.

"You mean you're different?" said Robby.

"Judge for yourself," said the Captain. "If a thief

broke into your house to take your things, that would be bad, wouldn't it?"

"Yes," said Robby, wondering where this was leading.

"But if a policeman saw the thief in there, and had to break in himself to arrest the thief and protect you, that would be good, wouldn't it?"

Robby thought. And nodded.

"But what if it wasn't a policeman who saw the thief, but just a public-spirited private citizen? Wouldn't it be just as good if *he* broke in and stopped the thief?"

Robby squirmed. What the Captain was saying *sounded* right. But something about it was wrong.

"But what if it wasn't really a thief he saw?" said Robby, after a long moment. "Maybe he ought to just go get a policeman, anyhow, because — "

"There isn't time," interrupted the Captain. "Let's say the policeman isn't on duty where he should be, or some such thing. What then?"

"Well," said Robby, doubtfully, "I guess . . ."

"Of course, you see the point now!" said the Captain. "Public-spirited people must come to the rescue of their neighbors. And that is exactly what we're here to do now: protect the people of our world against the Martians."

"Oh, but the Martians can't hurt us!" said Robby. "I've taken care of them in the tanks downstairs for a year, now, and — "

"How do you know?" broke in the Captain, thrusting his chin at Robby. "How do you know they can't hurt the world? What if they got loose in the seas and multiplied? And then came out on the land and overran the land? What makes you so sure they mightn't chase us right off the face of the earth?" He sat back, and his voice became smoother and less loud. "No, no, Robin — the thing to do is destroy the aliens before they destroy us." His eyes lighted up. "The world will thank us for it someday! But we need your help."

"Me?" Robby stared at him.

"Yes," said the Captain.

He got to his feet. "Just a moment while I lock the door. There are spies everywhere."

He went over to the door of the office to lock it, and Robby, glancing at the desk he had just left, had a wild idea. Sitting on the desk, he saw his father's video-phone. It looked, and almost was, like all the other extension phones spotted about the station. But Robby knew that this one was different in one small way. It was connected, not only to the regular telephone center in the communications room upstairs, which the Vandals had jammed, but also, by a special switch, to a government cable for official and top-secret calls dealing with the research animals. Robby glanced at the Captain. His back was still turned.

Hurriedly, Robby reached behind the phone to

flip the cable switch. Then he pushed a button. Now every word he and the Captain said would go out over the special cable. Robby could only hope that there was somebody at the other end to hear it and understand the situation he was in.

"There!" said the Captain, with satisfaction. "Tricky locks you have here." He sat down again and became suddenly brisk. "One of the most dangerous of the Martian monsters escaped recently from where some misguided scientists were examining it. We captured the monster, but it got away from us again. It's somewhere in the vicinity of this station, and we believe you may have seen it. Have you seen anything that looked like this?"

He passed a drawing across the desk to Robby. Robby took it. It was a picture of the sea badger all right, but the artist had made a number of changes in the Martian's appearance. Only the shape of the body was the same. Instead of the bony plates in the mouth, the drawing had dragonlike fangs; instead of the big digging hands, horrendous claws. The monster was shown crouched and snarling over a small, shrinking human being, a fierce expression on its face.

"Ah," said the Captain, who had been watching Robby closely. "I see you have. Perhaps you have also seen an Intelligence Bureau agent, a little man about your size?"

Robby said nothing.

"I see," said the Captain, at last. "Robin, it wouldn't be very wise of you to refuse to help us find those two. We're good friends to those who are friends to us, but we can be pretty terrible to our enemies."

"You can't make me talk!" Robby burst out.

"Yes we can," said the Captain, "but I don't think we'll have to." He turned halfway in his chair and pointed out the undersea window. "Is that dolphin a pet of yours?"

Beyond the glass, Balthasar — as he so often did — was stunting and turning, in hopes of luring Robby outside for a swim.

"I imagine you're pretty fond of him," said the Vandal captain, all the smiles and pleasantness gone from his face now. "Unless you help us find the monster and that agent, as I know you can, I'll arrange to have that dolphin netted and —"

He broke off. At first Robby could not understand why. Then he saw that the Captain was listening. He sat motionless at his desk, and his face under the freckles had gone quite pale. Robby listened, too.

After a second, he heard a voice. It was a voice distantly singing, and it sang a song that Robby had heard before:

*Lilli-bu-ler*
*Lero, lero;*
*Lilli-bu-ler —*
*Lero —*

# Rescued—and Trapped!

WHERE the song was coming from, Robby could not tell. He looked at the ventilator above the desk, he looked at the video-phone on the desk. He looked at the door of the closet, and he looked back at the Captain.

But the Captain had evidently made up his mind where the song came from. Slowly and quietly, he was sliding open a drawer of the desk, and, as Robby watched, he rose silently to his feet. On tiptoes he approached the door of the office, laid his hand on the lock, and noiselessly slipped it off. He put his hand on the knob of the door, ready to jerk it open.

In that second, the screen of the ventilator suddenly twanged and sprang outward into the room. Frantically, the Captain spun around, but before he could duck, the steak-sauce bottle — the one with

108

many-colored rings — came whizzing from the ventilator opening and shattered against his forehead.

The Captain dropped. And Mr. Lillibulero leaped lightly out of the ventilator opening.

"Now, Robertson," he said. "Quickly!"

He snatched open the door of the office, led Robby out, and locked the door behind them. He led the way out into the corridor at a run, past one startled Vandal, and up the steps to the top level.

"Hey!" cried the Vandal behind them. But they were already up the stairs, into the top level of the station, and Mr. Lillibulero was securing the heavy interlevel door. Robby turned to see a Vandal coming from the communications room and two more approaching from the opposite direction.

"Lock the top door, laddie!" cried Mr. Lillibulero. "Pay no mind to these others. Leave them t'me."

Robby darted toward the steps leading up to the surface platform overhead. The Vandal from the communications room made a wild grab at him, but Robby ducked under the man's arm like a greased eel and was up the stairs in a moment.

He grabbed for the lock to the surface hatch and shot it closed, expecting any moment to feel heavy hands upon him. But they did not come. When Robby turned around, he saw why. The Vandal had gone to help the others against Mr. Lillibulero.

It was one of the strangest fights that Robby had

ever seen. The lightest Vandal there weighed almost twice as much as Mr. Lillibulero, and there were three of them.

But it never pays to underestimate an opponent. On a certain paper in a certain filing cabinet in a certain top-secret office, there were listed (unknown to the Vandals) certain abilities of Mr. Lillibulero. And this list, in addition to mentioning a host of other things he was good at (pistol, rifle, bow and arrow, knife, boomerang), carefully noted that Mr. Lillibulero was highly proficient in the arts of boxing, wrestling, judo (and jujitsu), *savate* (including *chausson*, or *jeu marseillais*), and *karate*.

The first Vandal that reached him found himself

flipped head over heels, to land on the floor so hard
that all the wind was knocked out of him. The second Vandal was tripped up; and the third, falling
over the second, ran headlong into a right cross to
the jaw that dropped him in his tracks. The second
Vandal, struggling to his feet, met a judo chop on
the way up, and lay down again.

The combat was over.

Robby helped Mr. Lillibulero tie the hands of the
Vandals behind them. Meanwhile fists could be
heard pounding on the two doors: the one to the
level below, and the hatch to the surface platform
above. But those doors had been built to withstand
all the power of the sea, in case it should break into

the station and one level needed to be sealed off from another. The doors held.

By the time Robby and Mr. Lillibulero had finished tying them up, the Vandals were all conscious again, but quite unhappy. Mr. Lillibulero got them on their feet, marched them into the equipment room, and locked them in a closet.

"Now," said Mr. Lillibulero, turning to Robby, "to get off a wee message to the proper authorities."

In the communications room he sat down before the main board. In front of him were controls for the regular video-phone connection to the mainland, a bypass on the International Fisheries official tele-type, short-wave equipment for communicating with ships at sea and aircraft, and an automatic distress signal.

Mr. Lillibulero went to work on these controls. After a second, he sat back and looked at them all.

"Hmm," he said.

"What's the matter?" Robby asked.

"The matter, Robertson, now that y'ask," replied Mr. Lillibulero, "is that yon Vandals are still jamming the communications. I had hoped they'd have quit when they found no one here earlier. But they're still at it."

"You mean we can't call out?"

"I mean that."

Robby stared at the little man, feeling his stomach sink. He had been so glad to see Mr. Lillibulero, he had somehow jumped to the conclusion that now everything would be all right. It came home to him with a shock that things might not be all right, after all. In fact, they might be even worse, judging by the noise the Vandals were making, shouting and pounding on the door. It might be that the Vandals would be angry enough to do something desperate, once they had succeeded in breaking down one of the doors.

"But can't we do anything?" cried Robby.

"There are," said Mr. Lillibulero, "a number of things we might do. Most of them, however, such as running around in circles and tearing our hair whilst bemoaning our lot, would hardly be of much sairvice to us. On the other hand, there are two excellent things we *can* do."

"What?" said Robby.

"We can wait. 'Tis always good tactics when y'find y'rself losing to delay th'end as long as possible. There is no telling what may turn up, even in th'most hopeless situations. Also, we can think. Thinking is the gr-reat ability of man — that which separates him from the poor beasts of the animal kingdom. I would advise any person," said Mr. Lillibulero, with kindling eye, "I would advise him, when in a tight spot, t'think *first* and act *afterwards*, because there is no telling what he may think of if he gives himself the chance. Therefore, Robertson, let us sit down, make ourselves comfortable — and think while we wait."

Suiting the action to the word, Mr. Lillibulero found himself a comfortable chair across the room. Robby sat down in a chair opposite. For a long moment, neither one of them said anything, and the distant sound of the Vandals was the only thing to be heard.

"Uh — " said Robby, hesitantly, after a little while. "Is it all right to talk while thinking? Because I — "

"Y'have the floor," said Mr. Lillibulero, courteously. And then, seeing that Robby looked somewhat puzzled, he explained, "I mean, talk as much as y'want."

"Well, I just wanted to mention," said Robby, "that they're trying to burn down the door from the second level, or something."

The little man popped to his feet, hurried over to the door, and examined the cherry-red spot that had blossomed on its metal surface near the doorknob. He put his palm close to it, nodded, and then came back to sit down again.

" 'Tis only an ordinary welding torch," he said to Robby. "And th'door's made of a cerametal compound — which, in case y'dinna know, is a material developed originally for rocket nose cones to take the great heat of travel through the atmosphere. They'll not cut through it with that."

"Oh!" said Robby, suddenly remembering, "I maybe got a message out myself a while ago." And he told Mr. Lillibulero about his trick with the video-phone on his father's desk.

"Well done, Robertson," said Mr. Lillibulero, when he had finished. "Though I'd not count too greatly on rescue in the nick of time. 'Tis something that happens more often in books than in real life."

"I guess so," said Robby. He wiggled uncomfortably on the chair, "I'm — uh — sorry about the — well, you know — "

"The what?" asked Mr. Lillibulero.

"The octopus," stammered Robby.

"What octopus?"

"The octopus in the tunnel. I mean, I knew there was an octopus in there — "

"Octopi," said Mr. Lillibulero, sternly, "have never been one of my terrors . . . ah!" he said, breaking off sharply and fixing Robby with a penetrating eye. "You thought perhaps they might be?"

"Well, you see — " said Robby, going rather red in the face.

"Say no more," said Mr. Lillibulero. "There was no harm done. As it happened, when I got to a certain point in the tunnel, there was no octopus, but a hole dug by the sea badger. I swam down it until,

some long distance away, I came out into open sea
again. The Martian beast must have been attempt-
ing to tunnel until he came into another cave, hoping for food, as he would have found it on his own
world. Finding nothing, he dug down to the sea he
knew was there. When I came out the other end of
the tunnel, I did not know where I was, and so had
to come back by the same way as I went, to make
sure of finding you." He looked closely at Robby.
"However, when I got back to where I'd left you,
y'were gone."

"Well, I thought — "

"Y'need not tell me what y'thought," said Mr.
Lillibulero. "Perhaps we'll both be happier wi'me
not knowing."

"Oh no!" cried Robby. "What I mean is I thought
you had been trapped by the sea badger and that
it was all my fault for not telling you about the octopus. I thought something had happened to you.
And if I'd told you, you wouldn't have gone in after
the sea badger."

"Ah, indeed?" said Mr. Lillibulero, in a sharp,
jagged voice. His eyes were quite shiny. He stood
up and walked over to the communications main
board, where there was a box of tissues left by Robby's mother. He took a couple and blew his nose
vigorously. "Well, Robertson," he continued, re-
turning to his seat, "y'r feelings do y'credit. We're

none of us so perfect as we'd like to be, and it may be I'm a wee bit unreasonable myself sometimes. As for what I did, y'may put y'r mind to rest, it being my duty to follow th'beast at th'time, no matter where it chanced to lead me."

After which he cleared his throat very fiercely, glared at Robby, and seemed about to say something more. Then, abruptly, his expression changed and he went over to the door.

"What is it?" asked Robby, following him.

"I'm afraid it's our luck running out," said Mr. Lillibulero. He pointed to a spot of white in the center of the glowing red patch on the door. "They've found something hotter — possibly a pressure torch — and they'll be able to cut through after all." He crossed the room to the communications board and began hefting microphone stands and a heavy brass ash tray he found on a table. Finally, he unscrewed the base of a table lamp and held it in his hand.

" 'Tis a poor sort of club, but necessity is the mother of invention," he was commencing to explain to Robby, when the whole station seemed to explode with sound. The floor under their feet shivered, the walls rang, and the noise of great blows against metal jarred their ears. Robby and Mr. Lillibulero stared at each other. And then, without warning, the little man dropped flat and pressed his right ear against the floor under their feet.

"'Tis coming from below all right!" he cried at Robby over the noise. "At the base of the building, I'd say."

"Maybe it's — " Robby shouted, but his voice was lost in the noise.

"What?" cried Mr. Lillibulero, bounding to his feet.

"I say," yelled Robby — and the noise suddenly ceased, so that he found himself shouting in a quiet room. "I mean," he went on in a lower voice, "maybe it's the sea badger. I took a lot of Martian plants from our experimental tank and made a trail up to the station. I figured he was hungry and — "

"And the beast'll be trying to dig its way in right now!" snapped Mr. Lillibulero. "Listen t'them outside there!"

They could hear Vandal voices raised in excitement and alarm.

"Overside, all of you!" the voice of the Captain was roaring. Somebody objected. "Well, out the third-level lock then, if you can't get up to the platform! Rig the nets! I want that Martian, like the two in there, *dead or alive!*"

The tremendous banging began again. And for several minutes nothing could be heard.

"Back to the door! Burn it through!" was what came through to their ears when the sea badger paused again. "The others can get the Martian."

"Laddie!" snapped Mr. Lillibulero. "Now's our chance. Follow me!"

He was up the steps to the platform above in a flash, and had the locks on the hatch shoved back before Robby caught up with him. He shoved upward. Bang, went the hatch, up and open. And the two of them tumbled out on to the floor of the surface platform.

They emerged, it seemed, into the midst of a horde of Vandals. There were not merely two or three of the big men on the platform, armed to the teeth, there were six, or eight, or maybe even a dozen.

"Never mind me, lad!" cried Mr. Lillibulero, throwing himself among them. "Jump, Robertson! Over the side!"

Robby grabbed a lung, raced, and plunged. The soft water closed with a cool shock around him. He dived deep, intending to baffle his pursuers by slipping around the station and away. But to his dismay, he found himself surrounded by Vandals (there were, in fact, twenty-three of them in the water at the time, as he found out later), all with swimming lungs and shark knives.

They dropped the large underwater net they were rigging and turned, as one, to close in on Robby.

# Balthasar

BALTHASAR had spent a restless night since he had watched Robby go with the Vandals into the station. There was no good reason for this. Here was the station as it always had been, and there was Robby inside it. But, somehow, Balthasar did not like it. He swam past the window of Robby's bedroom and saw Robby inside. Robby waved to him, but still Balthasar felt uncomfortable. He even went so far as to swim down to the third-level lock and push the button that signaled he wanted to be let in.

A Vandal, thinking it short-circuited when he heard it ring, had shut off the sounding bell. But nothing happened. After getting no response at the lock, Balthasar surfaced several times at the edge of the platform, clacking his hard lips together and giving the hoarse, squeaky little cry of the dolphins. But only a Vandal standing alone on the platform stared at him rather foolishly each time he came up. The man made Balthasar uneasy, and the dolphin dropped back into the obscurity of the dark waters.

No, there was nothing wrong that he could see. But still Balthasar sensed there was trouble about.

He cheered up considerably when he saw the little man Robby had befriended swim stealthily up to the platform and sneak down the ventilator scoop when the Vandal guard's back was turned. But just after that there was a lot of noise from inside the station, and he felt uneasy again.

And then, a short while later, he was thrown into a panic when he saw the sea badger approaching.

Balthasar was afraid of the sea badger. It was strange. It was different. Who knew what it might not do? Balthasar expected the worst from it.

And almost immediately his expectations were justified. For the sea badger, which had been quietly eating its way along the sea bottom up to the station, suddenly went berserk.

It began to attack the station — Balthasar's station — with Balthasar's Robby inside!

Balthasar's first, automatic action was to streak around the station and down to the lock button to sound the alarm. After jabbing at the useless button for several frantic seconds, he shot away to peer in Robby's bedroom window. But Robby was not there. He whirled around the station, staring in all the windows. But Robby was not to be seen.

In absolute desperation, Balthasar dashed down to join battle with the sea badger itself. It was now inside the station, but to Balthasar's annoyance the Vandals were hanging a net over the hole where it had forced its way in.

There was only one thing to do, and that was to tear through the net. Balthasar slipped up to the surface to blow and fill his lungs with air. As he started down again, Robby plunged into the water from the station platform.

Robby's dive had taken everybody by surprise, including the Vandals in the water. Nevertheless, they dropped their net with no great alarm, knowing that there was no way he could escape them.

And then Balthasar hit them.

There is a reason why sharks and such creatures are not eager to tangle with dolphins. Even a small dolphin can flash himself through the water at high speed; and when he hits, he butts hard, with all the weight of his body, into the shark's soft side and belly. Also, he bites and twists as he hits, and his teeth, while not so terrible as the shark's, are not so small that a shark can take much of that sort of treatment and survive.

Balthasar burst into the midst of the Vandals like a lion into the middle of a flock of sheep. Luckily for them, he was more interested in getting to Robby as quickly as possible than he was in dealing out any damage on the way. Consequently, he merely bounced them aside, not injuring them too badly. He swirled to a stop before Robby, who grabbed thankfully at his reins, and they headed out again.

Once more Balthasar tore through the Vandals, and this completed the rout. The frightened Vandals swam desperately for safety — most of them for the platform, but a few for their own ship.

Those scrambling back on the platform joined the Vandals trying to grab Mr. Lillibulero. But Mr. Lillibulero was so small, so quick, so limber and spry, that he continually managed to wiggle out from their grasp.

It had only been a minute or so since Robby had dived overboard. Mr. Lillibulero, however, was still free, and since panic is contagious, the battle ended then and there. Suddenly all the Vandals could think of was to get away from whatever terrible peril now pursued them. And the fact that none of them really understood what he was running away from made no difference at all.

Meanwhile Robby, who had turned around after Balthasar had pulled him off to a safe distance, rose to the surface, saw what was going on, and came back to see if he could help Mr. Lillibulero.

He approached to find Mr. Lillibulero in control of the platform. Some Vandals were bolting for the interior of the station, while others were still clambering out of the water. But just then, looking beyond, Robby had a flashing glimpse of something more, something large and silver, coming quickly up to the station.

"A sh— " he started to yell, and then a wall of sea water stopped him as Balthasar plunged into a wave. Robby bobbed up immediately, shaking the water from his mask microphone.

"A ship! Mr. Lillibulero!" he cried. "A ship!"

Robby and Balthasar set off at top speed in the direction of the oncoming vessel.

Balthasar was fast, but the ship was faster. It slid across the surface on a cushion of air pushed out by thousands of tiny jets in its flat bottom. It was the Mexican government patrol boat under the command of Lieutenant Vargas.

The patrol boat reached the station and came to a skillful stop alongside. Robby and Balthasar were close behind.

Coastguardsmen in neat uniforms leaped to the platform as Robby scrambled out of the water, and was grabbed by his own worried father.

"Your mother," said his father about half an hour later, "your mother should be here in a couple of days, at the most. After we pulled the other sea badger through, she went to visit your aunt Sophie. What she'll say, I don't know. Probably it'll be my fault for not checking sooner to see if all was well. Did you watch the temperatures on experimental tank number seven?"

They were standing on the platform, and the coastguardsmen were herding the Vandal prisoners up from below and onto the patrol boat, where they would be taken under guard to the mainland for trial. The coastguardsmen had sprayed a soothing gas at them in order to capture them without hurting them, and they were very relaxed at the moment and sleepy, although they would return to normal when the effects of the gas wore off. Before Robby could answer his father, the Vandal captain came up out of the platform entrance, smiling dizzily. He was led aboard the patrol boat.

"A sad case," commented his father. "Still, there's always hope of reform. And who knows? Possibly, there but for the sake of marine zoology, go I. None of us can afford to look down our noses at any of them. Don't you think so, Lillibulero?"

"I do," agreed the little man, who was standing nearby with Lieutenant Vargas. " 'Tis not easy *not* to be a Vandal. Each man must take the responsibility of escaping the temptation for himself. Luckily, however, in this case no harm's been done to speak of."

"Fortunately not," agreed Lieutenant Vargas. "My men have secured the hole by which the Martian entered your experimental tanks. The creature will not be able to escape again. It's feeding quietly in there now."

"A thousand thanks," said Robby's father.

"It was nothing, I assure you," replied Lieutenant Vargas. He looked very trim and military with his white uniform and the neat black mustache on his handsome olive face. "The creature gave us no trouble. We should thank your son for cleverly opening the video-phone line and alerting us that this bunch was here."

Robby squirmed with pleasure.

"Well, at any rate, the sea badger seems quite happy in there with the other Martians," said Robby's father. "Possibly that's what it needed and wanted all along. A little bit of home. Probably quite gentle and friendly under ordinary circumstances. We're to keep it, I understand, for further study here. Of course, we'll rig a tank it can't break out of. Robby may yet have it eating out of his hand."

"You should have seen it fighting the killer whale," began Robby.

"Whatever you do, don't tell your mother about that!" interrupted his father, horrified. "Not for a day or two, at any rate. Not until she's had time to get used to having the sea badger around. You know how your mother is."

Robby nodded seriously.

"And, as I say, she will probably hold me responsible. Of course, to a certain extent, I am. I would have taken you with me, except that my government orders were explicit: to go alone to your grandfather's and help him try to save the life of the sea badger that was hurt when this one was stolen."

"This other Martian, it is well now?" inquired Lieutenant Vargas.

"Quite well, thanks. A rather bad cut on the head, but it's recovering nicely," answered Robby's father.

"The point is," he went on, "lacking second sight, I had no way of knowing the Vandals would head straight here. And anyway, I left you in the care of Lillibulero, the most capable man in the world."

"I would not say that," objected Mr. Lillibulero.

"I would," said Robby's father. "I've known you for years. I know what you can do."

"Ah, but you forget what I cannot do," said Mr. Lillibulero. "For instance, I cannot fight a killer whale bare-handed. No more can I capture half a hundred or so Vandals, nor put a leash about the neck of a Martian sea badger and lead it home. If y'must know, it was not me that brought Robertson alive and well through the last day and night, but Robertson and myself that somehow brought each other through." He cast a grim but approving eye on Robby. "Was that not so, Robertson?"

"It sure was, Dad!" burst out Robby, excitedly. "If it hadn't been for me, no telling what might have happened. I mean, I knew about the shoals here, around the station, and where to look for the sea badger. I rode Balthasar after the killer whale, and saw the sea badger and knew it was around for sure. I left the video-phone off the hook and switched on the secret cable line. I left the trail of food for the sea badger. I did it. If it hadn't been for me — "

Robby saw all three men looking at him with an embarrassed expression, and all at once he seemed to be sitting once more in his father's office with the red-bearded Vandal captain opposite. Once again he heard the Vandal captain talking about right and wrong, and twisting them around to put himself in the best position. And right now Robby heard himself doing the same sort of thing. He gulped.

"That is — I mean — " he said quickly, "it was really us. What I mean is — " and he looked at Mr. Lillibulero, "it was mostly him."

Mr. Lillibulero almost smiled. His frosty emerald eyes sparkled. Lieutenant Vargas *did* smile. And Robby's father beamed. As for Robby himself, he felt good all over, with a warm, spreading glow he had never experienced before. So that suddenly he had to do something to show it.

"And Balthasar!" he cried, running to the edge of the platform where the big dolphin curvetted in the waves. "Balthasar was more help than two of me!"

And Balthasar leaped clear of the water, twisting with joy. The praise meant nothing to him, but what meant all the world was the sound of his name called happily once more in the voice of his beloved young master.